DESTROY

THE BLADES OF ACKTAR

DESTROY  A NOVELLA

TRICIA MINGERINK

Sword & Cross
Publishing

DESTROY

The Blades of Acktar Book 3.5

A Blades of Acktar Novella

A Blades of Acktar Companion Novella

Copyright © 2016 by Tricia Mingerink

Published by Sword & Cross Publishing

Grand Rapids, MI

Cover by Sword & Cross Publishing

Map by Md Shah Alam on Fiverr

All rights reserved. Except for brief quotations in written reviews, no part of this publication may be reproduced, stored in a retrieval system, or transmitted in any form or by any means—electronic, mechanical, photocopying, recording, or otherwise—without prior written permission of the author. No AI Training: Without in any way limiting the author's exclusive rights under copyright, any use of this publication to train generative artificial intelligence (AI) technologies to generate text is expressly prohibited. The author reserves all rights to license uses of this work for generative AI training and development of machine learning language models.

This book is a work of fiction. All characters, events, and settings are the product of the author's over active imagination. Any resemblance to any person, living or dead, events, or settings is purely coincidental or used fictitiously.

All Scripture quotes are taken from the King James Version of the Bible as found in the public domain. To God, my King and Father. Soli Deo Gloria

LCCN: 2019907319

ISBN: 978-1-943442-19-5

*The LORD appeared to Solomon in a dream by night: and God said, Ask what I shall give thee.
And Solomon said...Give therefore thy servant an understanding heart to judge thy people, that I may discern between good and bad.*

And God gave Solomon wisdom and understanding exceeding much, and largeness of heart, even as the sand that is on the sea shore.

- I Kings 3:5-9, 4:29

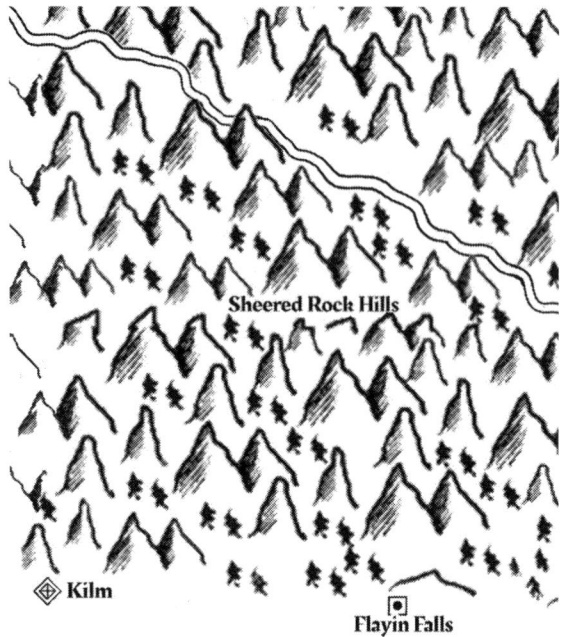

Sheered Rock Hills

◈ Kilm
▣ Flayin Falls

▣ Sierra
◈ Surgis

ACK

▣ Calloday   Nalgar Castle   ▣ Aven
         Dently ▣ 🏰
   Penning   Blathe ◈   ◈ Hakon
       ◈   ◈ Mackton
          Glarbon ▣
                        Keestone ▣
   ▣ Arroway
                    ▣ Lanson
         ◈ Dyman
                    ▣ Ably

- - - - - - - - - - - - - - - - - - -

VERDEN

1

Something slammed.

A hand grasped the back of seventeen-year-old Prince Keevan Eirdon's collar and yanked him from the linen closet where he'd been kissing a maid.

His uncle Laurence glared with burning eyes the color of a summer sky. "What do you think you are doing?"

Keevan gaped from him to the sixteen-year-old maid. She was crying, her hands shaking as she straightened her mussed hair. Cold doused Keevan. He'd let himself go too far.

What had he been thinking?

That's just it. He hadn't been thinking.

Uncle Laurence turned to the maid. "What's your name?"

"Ellenora." The maid shook harder.

Uncle Laurence's tone was gentle as he extended a hand. "If you would please come with me, my wife will look after you, all right?"

The maid's wide eyes glanced from Uncle Laurence to Keevan. Keevan wrapped his arms around his stomach. What had he done? He hadn't meant to go so far. He hadn't meant for any of this to happen.

With a shaky nod, the girl let Uncle Laurence steer her from the closet with a hand on her back. As they passed, Uncle Laurence sent Keevan a cold look. "Come."

Keevan didn't even try to disobey. He was a prince and technically he outranked his uncle—something he had used on occasion—but this time he couldn't dredge up that arrogance. Uncle Laurence wasn't in the mood to put up with him pulling rank.

As they rounded the corner into the guest wing, Keevan caught sight of Aunt Annita coming toward them, gripping Keevan's cousins Renna and Brandi on either side of her. Both of the girls were crying.

Keevan winced. This wasn't going to help Uncle Laurence's mood at all.

"What happened?" The tone in Uncle Laurence's voice was gentle, even if his eyes remained chips of ice.

"W-we made snowmen, but K-keevan whacked their heads off. Then he laughed at us." Eight-year-old Brandi scrubbed her eyes and glared up at Keevan. "He was very mean."

Twelve-year-old Renna sniffed, buried her face against Aunt Annita's arm, and mumbled, "We weren't supposed to tell."

Uncle Laurence's jaw flexed, and Keevan felt a tremor start in his own hands. He'd never seen Uncle Laurence this angry before. And that anger was directed at him.

But somehow, Uncle Laurence's voice remained soft

when he nudged the maid forward. "Annita, would you see to Ellenora, here?"

The sideways glance at Keevan seemed to give Aunt Annita enough information. Her eyes widened, and she let go of Brandi and Renna to wrap the maid in a hug. "Come with me, sweetheart."

When Aunt Annita, the maid, Renna, and Brandi disappeared into Uncle Laurence and Aunt Annita's suite of rooms, Uncle Laurence spun on his heel. Any gentleness deserted his angular face, leaving only hard lines around his mouth and eyes. Though not exceptionally tall or broad, Uncle Laurence's slim frame seemed to tower over Keevan.

With a firm hand on Keevan's shoulder, Uncle Laurence marched him down the hallway and into Keevan's room. Once inside, Uncle Laurence slammed the door and pointed at one of the plush chairs in front of the fireplace. "Sit."

Keevan stumbled across the room and flung himself into the chair, curling his legs beneath it. Was this what criminals felt like when they faced his father? Shame? Regret?

Had Keevan ever really felt shame before? He didn't think so. Not like this, anyway. He'd always tried to be like his older brother Aengus, always laughing off mistakes and whims as if they were nothing.

They always had been nothing. Whacking heads off snowmen. Shoving snow down the back of Renna's cloak. Teasing her. A few stolen kisses from the maids. Nothing really harmful. Nothing bad.

And he hadn't meant for this to be bad either. If Uncle Laurence hadn't found him, surely Keevan would've stopped before he'd gone too much farther, right? He wouldn't have actually hurt her.

Except that he had. She'd been crying and shaking, staring at him like he was some kind of monster. There must have been some moment when her hands started shoving against him and when she'd tried to tell him to stop, but he couldn't remember. He hadn't paid any attention to her, only to the pounding of his own pulse.

Uncle Laurence stalked across the room, picked up Keevan's Bible from the table beside his bed, and flipped through the pages. Striding to Keevan, he slammed the Bible into Keevan's lap.

Keevan jumped, barely registering where Uncle Laurence's finger pointed before he stepped back and crossed his arms. "Read it. Out loud."

Keevan swallowed. "H-husbands, love your wives, even as Christ loves the church."

Barely had the last word crawled out than Uncle Laurence snatched the Bible, leafed through a few more pages, and slammed it back in his lap. "And this one."

When Keevan finished that verse, Uncle Laurence repeated the process. Again and again, until Keevan lost count of the number of verses he read. Verses on love. On Christians being all one body. Husbands and wives. Treating each other as brothers and sisters in Christ. Fleeing temptation.

By the time Keevan finished reading a verse and Uncle Laurence didn't immediately snatch the Bible away, Keevan couldn't hide his shaking. He'd really messed up this time. Surely his father wouldn't let this slide. Not like he had everything else Keevan had done.

Uncle Laurence jerked a thumb at the door. All the verse

reading hadn't softened the hard edge of his voice. "Come. Let's talk to your father."

Keevan swallowed and pushed to his feet. He followed Uncle Laurence from his room, down the hallway, and outside into the Queen's Court. They trudged across the snow-covered paths, into the passageway that connected the two courtyards, and up the narrow staircase to his parents' rooms.

The cold bit into Keevan's nose, and he stuffed his fingers into his armpits. He hadn't grabbed a cloak, mittens, or scarf when Uncle Laurence had marched him outside. Then again, Uncle Laurence hadn't grabbed anything either. But perhaps he was still too angry to feel the cold at the moment.

As they neared the top, a clerk dashed out the door, nearly running into Uncle Laurence. The clerk paled and threw himself to the side. "S-sorry, sir. Your Highness." The clerk pressed himself to the wall and inched past Keevan.

Keevan realized, as the clerk dashed down the rest of the stairs, that he probably should've thought to move out of the man's way. Uncle Laurence had.

Uncle Laurence shoved open the door to Father's study without bothering to knock. Keevan tiptoed after him. His father hunched over a stack of paperwork on his desk under the window overlooking the cobblestone courtyard. His crown sat on another pile of papers. He didn't even glance up when they entered. "I told you. I'm not to be disturbed."

Uncle Laurence marched across the room, planted himself in front of the desk, and crossed his arms. "I caught your son kissing a maid in the closet. Again."

Father sighed and scratched his head. He still didn't look up. "Which one?"

"Keevan." Uncle Laurence didn't budge. "Leon, this has to stop. All of it. You can't keep letting your boys run loose like this. The country needs to trust the royal family's strength and integrity right now, not gossip about its scandals."

Keevan winced. Nalgar was still rife with the gossip of Aengus' last trip to a tavern.

"I don't see why it's such a big deal. Boys will be boys. You probably did your own amount of kissing in closets. I know I did. We have bigger things to worry about." Father finally looked up. Lines circled through the dark shadows under his eyes. He pushed the stack of paperwork toward Uncle Laurence. "Rovers struck Clarbon. Killed a few people and drove off part of the cattle herd. Another group of Rovers took over Dyman, and I'm going to have to send in the army to dislodge them. I'm receiving more reports of strange activity around Blathe, but Lord Felix denies anything is going on. And then there's..."

"This isn't something you can brush off." Uncle Laurence didn't even glance at the stack of papers. "She was in tears, and I'm not sure what would've happened had I not stumbled across them."

Keevan flinched. What would have happened? He wasn't sure he wanted to be that honest, not even to himself.

"Really, Laurence, I doubt it was as bad as all that. My sons are essentially good boys. They'll settle down once they grow up a little." Father remained seated, but a hint of anger colored his tone.

Apparently, Uncle Laurence didn't care. He leaned on the desk. "They won't grow out of it without guidance. Yes, it was as bad as all that. Something like this has to be punished."

Father shot to his feet. Red suffused his cheeks and up his face all the way into his hairline. "Don't tell me how to raise my sons! It isn't your place."

Keevan glanced around the room, but he didn't dare flee and draw attention to himself. He didn't want to hear his father and uncle argue. Especially not about him.

"No, maybe it isn't." Uncle Laurence's tone cut as sharply as the midwinter air outside. "But it is my duty to be concerned about my daughters, and I won't have them stay in a place where this kind of thing is ignored. My family will be leaving. Today."

Uncle Laurence spun on his heels and stalked from the room.

Father slumped back in his chair, scrubbing a hand across his face and eyes. When the sunlight glinted across his blond hair, Keevan caught sight of a few silver strands at his temple. When had his father started to get gray hairs?

When Father looked up at him, it was with tired, brown eyes. "Keevan, just...try to behave, all right? I can't deal with anything more right now."

Keevan bobbed a nod and took that as his permission to leave. He fled down the stairs, but halted in the passageway at the bottom and leaned against the wall. The stones sucked his body's warmth through his clothes, and his breath misted in the air, but he didn't care.

The weariness in his father's voice...the spark in Uncle Laurence's eyes...Keevan couldn't decide which was worse.

He hadn't really been all that bad, had he? It was just a little bit of kissing.

Except that he might not have stopped there if he hadn't been interrupted. He'd ignored her *no* simply because his desires were telling him *yes*.

A hand slapped against his shoulder. "What's going on? I just passed Uncle Laurence, and he looked like he'd swallowed a rattlesnake."

Keevan glanced up into Aengus' grinning face. "Uncle Laurence caught me kissing a maid in the linen closet. He wasn't happy about it."

"Is that all?" Aengus shook his head, scattering water droplets from the beard and mustache he'd begun to grow. "He'll get over it."

"Not this time." Keevan stuffed his hands under his arms. His fingertips were already going numb. He probably should go inside, but the cold seemed like a small form of punishment for what he'd done, since he wouldn't suffer anything else.

"He will. Besides, Uncle Laurence always acts a bit too perfect. We can't all be that good. Now, look at what I smuggled out of the kitchen." Aengus opened his cloak and pulled out a bottle from its hiding place under his shirt. The dark, amber liquid sloshed. "A whole bottle of the cook's whiskey. I found his new hiding spot. Why don't we slip back to my room and nip a few glasses?"

And those few glasses would turn into the whole bottle. It always did with Aengus.

Keevan found himself swaying forward. It would be so easy to follow Aengus and drink until his head buzzed and he couldn't help but laugh and smirk and joke as if none of this had ever happened. He'd probably end up telling Aengus the whole story, and after a few glasses of the whiskey, they'd both end up laughing about it. Just like they'd done many times before.

Keevan's stomach churned. What would Uncle Laurence's reaction be to that, if he caught them?

Except that he wouldn't. He, Aunt Annita, Brandi, and Renna would be leaving shortly. All because of Keevan.

"N-no. They'll be looking for us soon. Uncle Laurence and Aunt Annita are leaving, and they'll want us there to say goodbye." Keevan curled his toes in his boots, trying to keep them from going numb.

"They're leaving?" Aengus raised his eyebrows. "You weren't kidding that Uncle Laurence was peeved. All the more reason to get a few swigs in now. You know how long it takes to pack. They won't leave for hours yet. We'll have more than enough time. Besides, I'm now cold, and I need a few drinks to warm me up."

Keevan found himself pushing away from the wall before he caught himself. This was how it had always been. He could never say no to Aengus. Not when he'd offered Keevan his first swig of whiskey. Not when he'd challenged him to kiss a maid in the closet. Keevan always went along with whatever Aengus asked.

If he went this time, he'd continue just how he'd always been. Drinking. Luring maids into closets. And one of these days, he'd go too far with one or both of those things.

Or, he could stop. He could try to be better. More like Uncle Laurence.

"No, I just don't really want to right now." Keevan ducked around Aengus and hurried down the passageway. When he turned the corner, he broke into a run. Once inside the family wing of the castle, he had to dodge between the bustle of servants helping Uncle Laurence and Aunt Annita pack.

When he burst into his room, he slammed the door closed and sank into the same chair where he'd received Uncle Laurence's Bible verse lecture.

An hour later, he found himself bundled in his cloak, hat, mittens, and scarf, and standing in the few inches of snow that had yet to be shoveled off the cobblestone courtyard. The goodbyes between his family and Uncle Laurence and Aunt Annita had been stiff, and now they rode out of the castle without a backward glance, the maid and her family riding with them.

Twelve-year-old Duncan, Keevan's youngest brother, glanced up at Mother. "Why did Renna and Brandi have to go?"

Beside him fourteen-year-old Rorin also turned toward Mother. She sighed and wrapped her arm around Duncan's slim shoulders. In the afternoon light, the lines on her face seemed deeper, her hair a lighter blond. "An argument. But don't worry about it, all right, dearest?"

An argument. Keevan's stomach turned. Of course Duncan was too young to be told the full truth. Even Rorin wouldn't be told.

They couldn't ever find out that Keevan's actions had destroyed their family.

2

NEARLY A YEAR LATER...

Something warm and firm pressed over his mouth, shoving him down into his pillow. Keevan's eyes flew open, his heart jolting into a panicked rhythm.

A dark figure leaned over him, one knee pinning Keevan's body and one of his arms to the bed. Moonlight played across a slim face and dark hair. A knife winked in a raised hand.

A knife. What was going on? Keevan's heart pounded into his throat, sharp and hard as the knife glittering in the silver light. This attacker was raising the knife like...like he intended to kill Keevan.

Keevan couldn't seem to will his body to move. This couldn't be happening. Surely this intruder wouldn't actually kill him. This had to be a nightmare or one of his brothers playing a trick on him.

But his brothers would've been grinning and laughing by now.

Keevan stared into the intruder's face and met a pair of bright green eyes. Unable to speak with the hand over his mouth, Keevan put all his pleading into his gaze. *Please don't...*

The eyes hardened. The fingers tightened on the hilt. The hand pressed harder against Keevan's face.

A jolt shuddered through Keevan's body. There was no mercy in those eyes.

Keevan's pounding heart finally pulsed into his limbs and hands, giving him the strength to move. To fight. He writhed, but his free hand caught in the blankets. He couldn't reach his sword. He couldn't throw off this attacker, small as he seemed to be.

The knife sliced down.

Pain carved along Keevan's face and neck. He gasped. Something wet and sticky caught in his throat.

The pressure from the intruder's knee and hand left, but Keevan couldn't fight back. He shook with each partial, choking gasp.

He couldn't breathe. Blackness closed tighter around him.

He was going to die.

ADELAIDE CROFT TOTTERED DOWN THE CORRIDOR. WEEKS like this were the bane of the entire castle staff's existence. King Leon had called an emergency Gathering of the Nobles, and while the nobles discussed policy and politics, the staff tried to keep up with all the cleaning, laundry, and cooking such a large gathering required.

Addie's arms ached with all the scrubbing she'd done, and she'd finally finished getting the last of the dirt from the rugs in the hallway, just in time for the princes to tromp through with muddy boots again in the morning.

All she had to do now was check to make sure the fresh linens had been stocked in the linen closet for tomorrow morning, and she could finally head to her family's rooms in the servants' wing branching off the kitchen tower. If not for all the extra work, she would've finished her chores long before this.

The candles in the wall sconces were nothing more than flickering nubs, casting strange shadows against the paintings on the one wall and the doors lining the other side. The moon's light poured through the window at the far end beside the stairs. It had to be midnight or later. She'd have less than five hours of sleep before she had to be up again.

With a glance around, she quickened her pace. She wouldn't feel safe until she'd finished in the linen closet and gotten down the stairs. Mother had always warned her never to enter this hallway after dark. The princes, especially the two oldest, were known for liaisons with the maids, and there were rumors that not all of the maids had been willing.

She shivered. Surely none of the princes would be up and about at this time of night.

"Any sensible person would be in bed." The sound of her own whispered voice eased some of the tension. "I'll hurry. Mother will send out one of the boys if I'm not back soon, and they'd never let me hear the end of it."

She bustled into the linen closet, shutting the door until

only a crack remained between it and the jamb. For some reason, having the door between her and the hall made her feel safer, even if it wasn't much of a defense.

Of course, nothing was out there. Just shadows and her own imagination.

In the faint light from the wall sconces, Addie counted the bed linens stacked on the shelves around her, finding them mostly by feel in the near darkness.

Something in the hall outside the closet squeaked. Addie froze, her heart giving a strange jump-beat. Was someone out there? Maybe Prince Aengus or Prince Keevan prowled the corridors at night, waiting for some unsuspecting maid to wander by.

Should she stay here? Was this a good place to hide? Or would that be like a mouse waiting in the trap for the cat to come along?

She tiptoed to the door and peered out.

Something black moved at the far end of the corridor.

She stumbled back from the door. Her heart pummeled against her ribs. Someone was there. And if they were prowling the corridors at this time of night, they weren't up to any good.

Holding her breath, she peered through the sliver between the door and wall again.

The hallway remained utterly still. Empty. Shafts of moonlight speared through the high windows near the stairs.

Had she imagined the movement? And the noise? Wood often gave random squeaks and creaks as it shifted with the changing temperatures from day to night. Even a slight breeze could cause something to flex and groan. Perhaps her worked up mind had played a trick on her.

"Well, this is ridiculous." Wouldn't her brothers get a laugh out of her huddling in a closet over perfectly normal shadows?

She let out a breath and laid her palm against the door to push it open.

A black shape moved into the corridor. She stilled. Even her breath halted in her throat.

Another black shape followed the first, slightly smaller and thinner, though neither of them looked or moved like full grown men. More like boys.

Moonlight winked dully against something in their hands. Knives. What was going on? Who were these boys?

Two more black figures trailed behind. They set off silently down the hall she'd come from. Stalking into rooms. Ghosting out again. As one exited a room, a drop of something dark ran along the knife and fell, gleaming, to the rug. Addie pressed a hand over her mouth. Blood.

A cry rang out from somewhere outside. Far in the distance, shouting shattered the night.

The four figures dashed past her again, headed for the stairs. More shouting covered any noise their boots might have made.

She held her breath until they disappeared down the stairs and the corridor in front of the closet lapsed into stillness, except for the growing clamor outside.

She should stay where she was. That was the safest thing to do. The black-clad boys might come back. There might be more of them creeping about. She clapped her hands tighter over her mouth to keep from talking to herself and muttering her prayers out loud.

But these were the princes' rooms in front of her. She'd seen the boys exit with blood on their knives. She had to investigate, just to see if the princes were all right. If they were hurt, she could run for help.

She eased the door open a few inches and peered out. Nothing. Sticking her head out, she glanced around. Still nothing.

Creeping into the hallway, she darted for the door directly across from her. Prince Duncan's room. Her fingers halted on the knob. A maid didn't just enter a prince's room, especially not at night.

But Prince Duncan was only thirteen. He wouldn't be any threat to her, not like Prince Keevan or Prince Aengus might be if they caught her.

She'd poke her head in. Just long enough to see if he was all right.

But when she stepped inside, the sight on the bed halted her. She couldn't look away—couldn't comprehend—the blood, the wound, the child's still body. She couldn't even bring herself to move closer to check for life.

How could there be life with so much blood spilled? With a gaping gash like that?

Whirling, she dashed to Prince Rorin's room. More blood. Another body.

She trembled so much she could barely stumble toward Prince Keevan's room. Her stomach heaved, and she barely clenched her teeth in time to stop herself from vomiting onto the floor she'd spent hours cleaning earlier that night.

Collapsing to her knees, she braced herself against the

wall. What was the point of going in? Of seeing another mangled body?

They were all dead. Those boys in black had murdered all of them.

Why? When had the world tipped on its side and tangled in this madness? It didn't make sense. Nothing made sense.

Was that a sound? Addie swallowed and tried to hold back her gasps. Was she imagining things, or was there a rasping sound coming from inside Prince Keevan's room?

She couldn't go in. She couldn't face another dead body. That was the job for a soldier or a healer, not a nineteen-year-old scullery maid.

But if she didn't go in, and it turned out Prince Keevan was alive or there was something she could've done...

She had to check. She had to see this nightmare through to the end.

Forcing herself to her feet, she shoved the door open. The same sight assailed her. The prince's body on the bed. The glisten of blood in the moonlight.

The gurgling sound came again. The body on the bed twitched.

He was alive. This prince was alive.

Hands clenched, Addie approached the bed. Prince Keevan sprawled on his back, hands pressed to his throat. Something dark dripped through his fingers.

She should run for the healer. That's what she should do. But those killers had gone down the stairs to the exit. She might bump into them if she tried to go outside.

Prince Keevan turned his face toward her, his eyes wide as the moon outside the window. His mouth moved, but nothing came out but a gurgle and dribble of the same, dark substance.

Blood. She stumbled back from the bed. Her stomach curdled in her throat as the musty smell smacked her nose. The prince's eyes pleaded with her.

What was she supposed to do? She wasn't a healer. So much blood...she couldn't...

She didn't have a choice. Prince Keevan would bleed to death or suffocate if she didn't do something. There was no one else to help.

Clambering onto the bed, she knelt beside him. She grabbed a fistful of the sheet and yanked it free from the foot of the bed with the practice of many years of changing sheets and doing laundry. She pressed part of it against his face and throat. Warm liquid squeezed through the fabric and between her fingers.

Prince Keevan's eyes, wide and stricken, locked on hers.

"Breathe." She gritted her teeth. "Come on. You have to keep breathing."

His hands joined hers pressing the sheet against his face and neck. He coughed. More blood. Too much blood.

What should she do? She didn't know anything about healing besides the basics of try to stop the bleeding and wait for the healer to do the rest.

Was there anything she could do to help him breathe better? Should she turn him onto his side where the blood could drip out instead of into his throat? Or would that only make him bleed out faster?

Suffocate or bleed to death. She didn't have much choice.

She grasped Prince Keevan's shoulder and rolled him

onto his side, the same side as the wound. Would it be enough? It had to be enough.

She couldn't do anything else but pray. *Please keep him breathing.*

Somewhere outside, she could hear shouting. The Queen's Court below the window lit with torches. Footsteps pounded the corridor outside the room.

The door crashed open. A man dressed in a uniform, a captain by the silver patch on his chest, burst into the room, the light of his torch reflecting in his brown-gray hair. A squad of soldiers peered through the doorway behind him.

Addie froze. What did it look like to them? Her crouched on the bed next to the prince, her hands on his throat, blood pooling on the sheets around them.

Friends or enemies? Would they help? Or would they finish what that boy had started? And kill her too for witnessing it?

The captain's eyes widened, and he hurried to the side of the bed opposite of her. "He's alive." The words were half a question, as if the captain couldn't believe what he was seeing.

"Yes! Please help!" Addie didn't dare move. Prince Keevan's eyes were closed now, and she wasn't sure he was conscious. The only way she knew he was alive was the choked gasps shuddering into her fingers. "Someone tried to kill him, and I don't know why or what's going on or…"

The captain snapped upright and spun on his heels to face his men. They had crowded into the room, and now Addie counted six of them. The captain's hard gaze swept over them. "What you see here and what we are about to do, you must swear never to reveal to anyone. As of right now, the life of the last prince of Acktar rests on our hands."

The six soldiers rested their right hands across their chest. A chorus of "we solemnly swear" rang into the room.

With a curt nod, the captain pointed at one of the men. "Oran, see what you can do for the prince."

"Yes, sir." The soldier approached the bed and leaned over the prince next to Addie. "Let me see."

Addie eased her hands away from the prince's throat. The soldier peeled back the layers of sheets, exposing the gaping slash across the prince's face and down onto his neck.

Her stomach twisting, Addie turned away. Even the glimpse she'd seen had been too much. She closed her eyes, concentrating on the captain's voice as he ordered soldiers to guard the hallway, fetch a length of rope, smuggle a horse out of the castle, and fetch the body of a man called Theodor Kester. Addie could only guess how the captain knew that particular man was already dead or why his body was needed.

A hand rested on her shoulder, and she started, jerking away.

The soldier was peering at her. "What's your name?"

"A-Addie. Addie Croft. I'm a scullery maid." She bit her tongue. The soldier didn't need her whole name and life's story.

"Addie, nice to meet you. I'm Oran. I'm going to need an extra pair of hands to save the prince's life. Can you help me?" The soldier's smile softened the hard lines of his angular face. The shafts of moonlight carved shadows under eyes and hair that looked dark in the uncertain light.

Addie found herself nodding. What else could she do

but agree? There was no one else, and if the captain's insistence on making his men swear to secrecy was any indication, she wouldn't be leaving anytime soon. "What do you need?"

"Pull the drapes, then light a lamp. I'll start a fire. The bleeding has to be stopped, and as much as I hate to do it, the wound will have to be cauterized. I don't have a needle and thread with me." Oran sliced off a section of the sheet and wound it around the prince's neck and face. The white fabric stained red within moments.

Addie reached into her pocket. She could hear her mother's voice ringing in her ears: *A good maid always has a needle, thread, and a few buttons with her at all times. You never know when you have to mend something before the noble folk notice.* "I...I have my sewing kit with me. Would that needle work?"

"Yes, it should. Light the fire anyway. I'll stitch the section on his face, but the part on the neck will still need to be cauterized. It's bleeding too much."

Addie slid to her feet and dashed from window to window, yanking the heavy curtains closed. As she slid the last one shut, the room plunged into near total darkness, lit only by the glow of moonlight around the edges of the curtains.

A scraping sound came from the near the fireplace, accompanied by the flash of a spark.

Addie fumbled in her pocket for her flint and tinder—another of the things her mother admonished her to keep on her person at all times—and located the lamp on the bedside table. In the dark, it took her a few tries to get the spark to set the oil-soaked wick on fire, but it finally blazed.

Oran would need water to wash the wound before all the

stitching and cauterizing began. Addie fetched the water pitcher and basin—the same pitcher she'd filled only a few hours before—and returned to the bed.

Oran already leaned over the prince, peeling back the layers of makeshift bandaging. "Good. Bring the water over here."

How much more blood could the prince lose? Addie swallowed, set the basin on the table, and filled it with water. Locating the soldier's knife, she cut several chunks from the sheet.

She did her best to hold her stomach in place while Oran cleaned the wound. The stitching and cauterizing were only worse. By the time Oran wrapped more slices of sheet around the prince's neck, the captain was pacing by the door and Addie was one dribble of blood away from losing her stomach completely.

Oran straightened. "He's ready to be moved."

"Good." The captain peeked out the door and opened it. Two soldiers strode in, carrying a limp body between them.

Addie pressed herself against the wall, and looked away while the captain tugged a pair of trousers onto Prince Keevan. When she peeked back again, the captain slung Prince Keevan's still form over his shoulders and the soldiers dumped the body onto the bed. A gash ran across the body's throat.

One of the soldiers saluted the captain. "Sir, most of the fighting is over. Lord Respen Felix is parading the king's body about the courtyard, claiming victory. It won't be long before he sends men to retrieve the princes' bodies."

"Understood. I want the three of you to finish up here. Lengthen the gash onto his face, and make sure he is so smeared with blood no one will be able to distinguish him from the prince. Clean up anything we might have left out of place. Make sure you are long gone before they come for the body. There can't be any suspicion that the body they find isn't Prince Keevan's."

Addie sagged against the wall behind her. This went beyond madness. This was...she wasn't sure what it was. Yesterday, the world had been unchanging. The sun rose on the same world it had seen when it set.

But tonight...tonight had changed everything. The dawn tomorrow wouldn't be the same dawn she'd seen every other day of her nineteen years.

The captain swung toward her. "Addie, was it? Come with me."

She hurried to catch up as the captain strode from the door, Prince Keevan draped over his shoulder. In the corridor, they passed the soldier on watch and nodded at him.

At the base of the stairs, they stepped around the fallen bodies of a group of soldiers that had been set to guard the family wing of the castle.

After peeking out the door, the captain led the way outside into the Queen's Court. The moonlight shone along the patch of grass, the surrounding bluestone path, and the fountain trickling silver water. Men dashed about, and Addie couldn't be sure they were friends or enemies.

The captain set off at a jog along the perimeter of the Queen's Court, mostly sticking to the shadows beside the long gallery. Addie hurried to keep up. At the guest apartments set into the outside wall of Nalgar Castle, the captain ducked into a back door and dashed upward to the second floor.

Here, wails filled the corridor. Addie caught glimpses of some of the highborn ladies, swathed in robes and their hair hanging limp and untended, clinging to each other and sobbing. A few bodies sprawled across the rugs, and someone had thoughtfully tossed blankets over their still forms.

The captain nudged her. "Cry and grip his body like you're grieving. Make sure his face is covered."

Addie swallowed and pressed her face against the back of Prince Keevan's nightshirt. Cry? Could she cry on demand? She closed her eyes and dredged up the images she'd seen tonight. The young Prince Duncan's body so brutally murdered. Prince Keevan's choking, which still continued beneath her ear. All the blood. Too much blood.

What if this was one of her brothers? What if Brennen or Samuel lay under one of those blankets?

A cold settled into her chest. Her family. She'd been so focused on the tragedy happening to the royal family it hadn't occurred to her that her family was also in danger. Surely those black-clad assassins wouldn't attack a family of maids and stable boys, would they? The murders were only confined to the royal and noble wings of the castle. Only to those who really mattered.

Mama. Papa. Her brothers and sisters.

Tears pricked her eyes, and she forced a moan from her chest.

The captain set out down the corridor again, this time at a shuffling pace, his head hanging. Addie hunched over Prince Keevan's head and back, doing her best to sound distraught. A few of the noble women and their servants glanced their way, but only briefly.

That was the whole point. If the captain had barreled down this passageway looking like he was in a hurry, he would've drawn attention. But an army captain with a grieving girl and a dead body drew no more attention than any of the other crying, sobbing, wailing, weeping people around them. No one even looked at Prince Keevan, as if they couldn't bring themselves to confront yet another death.

At the far end of the corridor, the captain glanced around, then ducked into a curtained alcove. Addie followed a moment later.

The soldier who'd been sent for a rope waited next to the open window, the rope slung over his shoulder. When he spotted the captain, he stiffened and saluted. "A rope as ordered, sir. Arlo is below. He was only able to smuggle out one horse."

The captain sighed, then strangely enough, glanced at Addie. "I see. We'll make it work." He laid Prince Keevan on the windowseat, turned to Addie, and gripped her shoulders.

She stiffened at the weight of the captain's hands. What else would he want from her? She'd helped with Prince Keevan. She'd done more than her job. Now, everything in her coiled to dash to her family's rooms in the servants' quarters and see if they were all right. They were probably worried sick over her. Would her papa and brothers go looking for her? What if they ran into one of those assassins?

"Addie Croft, I need to beg your help once again. With only one horse, someone will have to ride double with the prince, and to keep from burdening the horse overmuch, the person has to be small and light."

She might be a scullery maid, but even she was smart

enough to see that between her and the men facing her, she was by far the lightest and smallest. "B-but I don't really know how to ride a horse or where to go or…"

"If the prince wakes, I'm sure he'll help. But I can't trust anyone other than my six men and you. You're all we have." The captain tightened his grip on her shoulders. "I wouldn't ask if I thought there was a better way. But more weight on the horse would only slow it down, and right now, the prince's life depends on speed."

Prince Keevan's life depended on her. No, all of Acktar depended on her.

She couldn't do this. This was ridiculous to even consider. She was just a scullery maid. Daughter of a long line of scullery maids. Plots and murders, destinies of kingdoms, all things for leaders and royalty to worry about.

But the king was dead. The whole royal family was dead except for the prince lying before her fighting for each breath through his damaged throat. If the wailing and grief in the corridor behind them was any proof, then many of the nobles who'd come for the Gathering were also dead.

There was no one else. Just her.

On a night like this, perhaps it made sense. If the world could be turned so upside down, perhaps a scullery maid could become important.

Tonight, men had died trying to protect the royal family. She could do no less than her duty for her prince. She forced herself to stand straighter. "All right. Where do you want me to take him?"

The captain glanced toward the window. Deep night wrapped around the castle, the stars faded in the brilliance of the moonlight. "Prince Keevan's uncle and aunt live in

Stetterly, but I doubt the prince would survive the five or six day ride. There are several towns within a day from here, but I wouldn't dare trust any of them. Not yet." The captain sighed and turned back to her, lines etched into his face. "Right now, the only town I'd trust besides Stetterly would be Walden. The heir of Walden, Lord Henry, is good friends with Lord Faythe of Stetterly. Surely he and his father remain loyal to the prince, if anyone still does."

Walden. Addie tried to picture the map of Acktar she'd glimpsed hanging on various walls in the castle. Too bad she'd never paid much attention to them. She'd never set foot outside Nalgar Castle before. Her parents had never set foot outside Nalgar. A tremor started in her knees. "How do I get to Walden?"

The captain produced a compass and held it flat on his palm. When the needle halted, he lined it up with the marking for north. He pointed at a marking between the north and east lines. "Head in this direction, and you'll reach Walden. Avoid all other towns and the roads. You can't be seen. The town of Walden lies where the Spires Canyon meets the foothills of the Sheered Rock Hills. If you miss the town, you can always either follow the foothills east or the canyon north until you reach it."

At least she'd know if she missed her mark or traveled too far. All she had to do was follow that little tick mark on the compass. She shivered. If she messed up, she and the prince would wander the endless prairie, lost until some traveler stumbled across their bones.

The captain gave her a few more instructions on picking a point on the horizon to make sure she stayed in a straight line and how to avoid being seen. "Do you understand?

Repeat my instructions and show me the mark you have to follow on the compass."

Addie pointed at the mark and repeated his words.

Apparently she got it right, because the captain nodded and pressed the compass into her hand. "When you reach Walden, tell no one but Lord Henry who you have with you."

"How will I get him to see me? I'm just a scullery maid." Addie slipped the compass into her pocket with her sewing kit and flint.

"Tell him you have a message for him from Captain Uriah Stewart at Nalgar Castle. He won't recognize my name, but he will probably see you, if only out of curiosity." Captain Stewart reached for the rope and looped it around Prince Keevan. "As far as I know, I'm now the highest ranking commander at Nalgar. All the generals were killed."

Addie pressed her fists against her sides. Truly no one was safe at Nalgar Castle. Not in this chaos. "My family. They'll be worried about me."

Captain Stewart finished tying the rope onto Prince Keevan. He and the soldier lifted the prince over the windowsill and lowered him down the wall. "My men and I will stay here as long as we can to help others escape and tend to a few details. Tell Lord Henry I will send the survivors of the army and those still loyal to the royal line to Walden when I can help them escape."

Addie nodded and stepped aside while Captain Stewart and the soldier lowered Prince Keevan down to the waiting horse and soldier. She ran all the instructions through her head again. Remember the correct mark on the compass. Don't tell anyone about the prince except Lord Henry, heir to Walden.

Too soon, the rope returned, and she looped it around herself. Climbing onto the windowsill, she balanced on the ledge. The prairie flowed dark into the star-specked horizon, vast and empty. Could she manage to find her way to Walden all by herself?

"Remember to hobble the horse at night. You know how to saddle it, right?"

Addie craned her neck to look over her shoulder at Captain Stewart. The rope cut into her ribs. "Yes."

Well, she was pretty sure. Her brothers had shown her how to do it. Once. A long time ago, before she'd started her job as a scullery maid.

Captain Stewart flexed his fingers on the rope. "Get as far from Nalgar as you can before you rest. I don't know if Lord Felix will send out parties searching for those who might have fled."

"All right." No, not all right. Not all right at all. But Addie nodded and pushed off from the wall anyway.

The rope cinched under her legs, as if she sat in the rope swing her brothers had once rigged in the castle stables before the head stablehand caught them. She gripped the rope and closed her eyes. This was a whole lot higher than the hayloft.

She sank foot by foot, her back sliding against the rough stones of the castle wall. A particularly sharp one scratched her arm.

But she didn't open her eyes or release her grip on the rope. She'd rather take the pain of bumping over the stones than risk losing her balance and falling.

"I got you, miss."

She peeled her eyes open. Her feet dangled only a few

inches over the ground, and a blond-haired soldier gripped the rope above her head as if to steady it for her. Clambering free of the rope, she dropped to the ground and tottered over to the horse.

Prince Keevan already slumped over the saddlehorn, a rope running around his waist tying him to the saddle.

If the soldier wondered why Captain Stewart was sending a random girl along with Prince Keevan, he didn't mention it. He simply boosted her up behind Prince Keevan and handed her the reins.

The horse sidestepped beneath her, as if uncomfortable with her added weight. Addie gripped the rope around Prince Keevan's waist and tried to peer around his shoulder to see the horse's head.

The soldier grabbed the horse's bridle and patted its neck. "I got what supplies I could. Sorry it isn't much."

"It'll be fine." Not really. Addie didn't have a clue what she was doing, but for some reason, everyone seemed to think she'd be fine. She fumbled in her pocket and pulled out the compass. Holding it flat on her hand, she waited until the needle stopped moving, then fixed her eyes on the hill in the distance that lined up with the correct mark. With her direction set, she stuffed the compass back into her pocket and gripped the reins and rope. "I'm ready."

"Our prayers ride with you." The soldier stepped back, let go of the bridle, and swatted the horse's rump.

If not for her grip on the rope, Addie would've tumbled right off the back of the horse. As it was, Prince Keevan's head flopped back and clunked against her forehead.

The horse charged into the star-strewn night and waves of moon-painted grass. She was so busy hanging on, trying to keep the horse going in the right direction, and steadying Prince Keevan's head, that she missed her chance to look back at Nalgar Castle.

Her home had disappeared behind her, and she hadn't even had a chance for goodbye.

3

Keevan woke to pain slicing across his face and neck. He blinked, but something white fluttered over one of his eyes, blocking the sight of the clear dome of blue sky far above him.

The taste of blood filled his mouth, but fire ripped apart his throat when he swallowed. He groaned, but nothing but a wispy gurgle came out, along with another shaft of pain.

Why had this happened? Keevan squeezed his eyes shut. It was all so random. A black-clad stranger broke into his room and tried to kill him. Why? Why?

What about Keevan's family? Another pain, deeper than the gash across his face, stabbed through his chest. Father. Mother. Aengus, Rorin, Duncan. Had the black-clad stranger hurt any of them?

But if they were fine, then what was he doing under this open sky with a rough blanket wrapped around him?

He couldn't think about it. His family had to be all right.

Some of them had to be. Perhaps he was the only one targeted, and this was the best way to keep him safe.

Turning his head shot pain through his face and neck, and he could only manage a few inches before the pain became too much.

Out of the corner of his eye, he spotted a girl sleeping a few feet away. She curled in a ball, the wool blanket cocooned around her so only her face and mass of brown hair peeked over the edge. A strand of hair fluttered each time she huffed out a breath.

She'd saved his life. That was the only thing he could be certain of this morning. He'd been alone, choking on his own blood and dying, when she'd appeared, her dress and hair sparkling with moonlight as she leaned over him. Almost like an angel, until her hands pressed pain into his wound.

He didn't even know her name.

What was he doing with her? He glanced around, but he couldn't see anything else other than a single horse wandering a few yards away. If he'd been sent away, where were the guards? What in Acktar was he doing in the middle of the prairie with no one besides a girl?

She snorted, rolled, and bolted upright. Her hair mashed against her head on one side and stuck out on the other. She scrubbed her eyes and stretched, pulling the linen of her brown dress taut around her body. He should look away, but he couldn't seem to find the energy...or the will power.

No, he did have the will power. He'd spent a year trying not to be the same boy he'd been.

He tore his gaze away and focused on her face, on the red

sleep lines etched into her cheek and the way her nose curved upward at the end.

With one last groan, she glanced at him and froze, one arm still stuck in the air, the other crooked behind her head. A red tint blotched across her nose and cheeks. She lowered her arms and tugged on her dress to straighten it. "Good morning, Your Highness. Did you sleep all right? How're you feeling?"

He opened his mouth and tried to force his throat to form words. Pain speared the back of his throat. Nothing more than air hissed out.

He couldn't talk.

Had that assassin's knife stolen his voice? Had he survived only to live like this the rest of his life? Silent?

"You look a little better. And you aren't choking and gagging anymore. That's a good thing." She scooched closer and leaned over him. Strands of her brown curls fell on his face, and he found himself staring up at...he yanked his mind back from the direction it had been headed. He had to be better than this.

Her bottom lip stuck out in what he could only guess was a grimace. "I should get a proper bandage on that. Maybe the saddlebags have a medical kit."

She stood and careened to a horse cropping on grass a few yards away. Hopefully she knew more about tending wounds than he did. She returned with the entire saddlebag. Plunking it on the ground next to him, she rifled through it. "Good, there's food in here. Though I doubt he can eat it, and I can't risk a fire. He's probably not hungry anyway. Let's see..."

She talked to herself. Perfect. Keevan squinted. Had she

forgotten he was here? Her constant muttering was already getting annoying, especially since he couldn't interrupt her.

Still nattering to herself, she yanked out a wad of bandages and a jar that looked like it might contain salve. Kneeling next to his face, she tugged on the fabric.

Pain tore across his face. He sucked in a breath and knocked her hand away. So much for knowledge of healing. Why couldn't she have been the castle healer? Or the healer's trainee?

She rocked back on her heels. "That's not going to work. Maybe water will help. It works on dried eggs." She shot to her feet and dashed toward the horse.

Now his face was dried egg? Keevan could think of a dozen people he would rather have with him than this...maid.

She returned, carrying a canteen. Her mouth and eyebrows puckering into frowns, she poured water across the bandage stuck to his face. As she tugged on the damp bandages, he squeezed his eyes shut. He couldn't even cry out at the pain.

"Sorry, sorry. I know this hurts. I'm so sorry."

Her babbling grated, but he didn't have the voice to tell her to stop nor the strength to press his hand to her mouth. At least his annoyance distracted him from the pain of ripping scabs.

"Last piece...here we go...got it!" The girl held up a bloodied scrap of what looked like bedsheet. When she glanced down at him again, her face drained of color. "Eww...I can see..." She jumped to her feet, dashed a few yards away, and crashed to her knees in the tall grass, her shoulders and back heaving.

Of course she'd have a weak stomach. He tried to peer down at himself, but he couldn't see much of his face or neck. Just a patch of blurry red at the edge of his vision when he craned his eyes downward. He could only imagine what she'd seen to set her to gagging.

After several minutes, she straightened, her fists clenched tightly at her sides. She stalked to him and knelt. "All right. I can do this. I don't have a choice, do I?"

Neither did he, apparently. He tried to hold still as she spread some kind of salve over his face and neck, laid a thick pad of linen bandages over the wounds, and wrapped part of his head and neck with more linen.

She gave him water and set to work packing their things. "We need to get moving. We can't risk that someone might be following us."

If only he could ask where they were going.

If only he could ask why.

If only he could speak.

He could refuse to move. For all he knew, she was kidnapping him or she was in league with that green-eyed boy in black.

Except she had saved his life. And right now, she was his only means to get somewhere, wherever that somewhere happened to be. He simply had to trust her.

He pushed himself onto his elbows. His head spun.

The girl crashed to her knees beside him. "Be careful. Are you sure you should get up?"

He ignored her and managed to push himself all the way into a sitting position.

"Fine. I guess you might as well get up. I was wondering how I'd get you onto the horse all by myself. Though, you'd better not pass out." The girl gripped his arm and yanked like she intended to rip his arm off.

Keevan struggled to his feet, the tilting in his head getting worse. He squeezed his eyes shut and gripped the girl's arm until some of the dizziness halted.

Opening his eyes, he staggered to the horse and gripped the halter to keep himself standing. His stomach heaved with the pain pounding through him. In all his life, he'd never felt this truly awful before.

Was this God's punishment on him? Keevan had used his looks, his voice, to lure that maid into kissing him. Maybe God was punishing Keevan for that now, since Keevan's father had never bothered doing so. A fitting punishment. No more good looks. No more fine words and witty charm.

The girl rolled their blankets into neat bundles and set them next to the saddlebags. When she'd gathered everything, she placed the saddle blanket onto the horse's back. The horse switched its tail and shied as far as its hobbled front legs would allow. Her mouth set in a line, the girl gripped the saddle and heaved it from the ground. The tendons in her neck straining, she could barely lift the saddle past her waist, probably because she was trying to lift it only by the saddlehorn.

Keevan reached for the saddle, staggered, and gritted his teeth. He couldn't pass out. Not now. This girl would never be able to heave his limp body onto the horse.

Gripping the back of the saddle, he helped her swing it onto the horse's back. Pain burst across his face, and next thing he knew, he was on his knees on the ground, gagging and gasping for breath.

"Are you all right? Please don't pass out on me again." The girl shook his arm, rattling his teeth.

If she kept shaking him like that, he might pass out sooner rather than later.

With her help, Keevan managed to climb back to his feet. Gritting his teeth and fighting his swirling vision, he did his best to position the saddle correctly. Grasping the girth strap, he tried to pull it tight, but his arms trembled.

The girl took the girth strap from him and pulled it tight. When it came time to tie it off, she started muttering again, fiddling with the leather strap.

Keevan gripped the saddlehorn and shook his head. If he wasn't about to collapse, he'd let go of the saddle and show her the correct way to tie it off.

After a few attempts, the girl finally got it right, mumbling something about how her brothers would be proud of her.

Brothers. Where were Keevan's brothers and parents? Keevan swallowed and nearly buckled under the agony that ripped through his neck. Still, that agony was small compared to the tearing in his chest.

He couldn't think about them, especially since he didn't know what had happened to them. For all he knew, they were all right.

The weight in his stomach told him they weren't. Nothing was all right.

Between the two of them, Keevan and the girl managed to get the horse's bridle on and strap the saddlebags and blankets onto the horse's back.

When they were packed, Keevan's face and neck throbbed, scattering black spots across his vision. He swayed and gripped the saddlehorn. Would he be able to drag himself into the saddle?

He didn't have a choice. He grabbed the saddlehorn and the back of the saddle, stuck his foot into the stirrup, bounced on the other, and heaved himself upward. He almost made it, but he didn't have enough strength for the last few inches.

The girl shoved against his back, and Keevan fell into the saddle, gasping. Pain tore across his face. The prairie and the horse's ears blurred.

"I'm sorry, Your Highness, but I think it would be best if we tied you to the saddle. If you pass out, I'm not sure I'll be able to hold you on." The girl held up a length of rope, biting her lip as if she wasn't sure how he'd react.

He nodded as much as he could, and even that much movement slashed pain down his neck.

She wrapped the rope around his waist and the saddlehorn. He tried to help her as much as he could, but his hands were shaking, too weak to even tug the knot tight.

After he was securely tied on, the girl stuck her foot into the stirrup and scrabbled up behind him, settling into a spot nestled in the blanket rolls and saddlebags. Instead of gripping him around the waist, she curled her fingers into the rope holding him on. "Do you want me to have the reins, or do you have them, Your Highness?"

He flexed his fingers around the reins. Until he passed out, he'd direct the horse. It was one thing he could control. He swiveled as much as he could and tilted his head at her, hoping she took the hint. What direction were they supposed to be heading?

"Did you want something, Your Highness?"

He waved a hand at the prairie around them, then pointed back at her. If he could talk, then he could simply ask her. Opening his mouth, he tried to get a word out, but nothing came besides a wisping croak.

"Are you all right? Is your face hurting worse? What do you need?"

He gritted his teeth. Couldn't this fool girl figure out he was trying to ask for directions? Nudging the horse, he turned it in a circle, glanced at her, and shrugged.

"Oh! You don't know where we're going, do you? I guess you were kind of unconscious for that part. We're headed to Walden." She dug into her pocket and pulled out a compass. After holding it flat on her palm for a few minutes, she pointed over the horse's right shoulder. "That way. This is going to be so much easier now that you're awake. You can guide the horse while I check direction, and I don't need to worry about holding you steady or checking that you're still breathing. I was so worried you'd just stop breathing on me, and I wouldn't know what to do, and after all we went through to get you out, you'd still die on me."

Keevan sighed and nudged the horse in the direction she'd indicated, focusing on an especially large tuft of grass as his marking point to keep himself headed in a straight line. He probably shouldn't be bothered by her chatter. If he couldn't talk, she might as well fill the silence.

The silence was the worst of all.

4

Addie could barely keep her eyes open when their horse staggered over a rise overlooking a lighted town. She checked her compass in the light of the waning moon. If she'd steered them in the right direction, then this was Walden. Against the deep purple horizon, cliffs and mountains rose deep and black.

She'd pushed them with too little rest, but Prince Keevan's condition had deteriorated throughout yesterday and today. He sagged in the saddle, held on only by the ropes she'd tied around him. Last she'd checked, he'd been far too hot, his wound inflamed. She didn't have the skills to help him, and Captain Stewart had been clear to trust only Lord Henry.

She rode through the nearly deserted streets and pointed their horse toward the stone manor house rising at the end of the road. As she turned into the open space in front of the manor's main door, a guard stepped out of the shadows and grabbed her horse's halter. "Where do you think you're going, miss?"

"I need to see Lord Henry Alistair right away. It's urgent." Addie gripped the horse's reins tightly. In front of her, Prince Keevan sprawled onto the horse's neck. He must have lost consciousness some time ago. She didn't have time to waste arguing with a guard. "Please. I must see him at once."

"Lord Henry has no wish to be disturbed at this time of night, especially not with trivial matters." The guard tugged on her horse's reins.

"This man is wounded. I can't wait." She waved at the prince. If only she could tell the guard who he was. Then the guard would jump to attention. But she didn't dare tell anyone except Lord Henry Alistair.

"Bring him to the healer in town. It's none of Lord Henry's concern."

"I bring news from Nalgar Castle. For his ears only." She had to convince this guard somehow.

The guard snorted and shook his head. "Like the king would send a little snip of a girl to carry his messages. Now go find a place in town. You can try again in the morning." He yanked on her horse's reins, turning it toward town.

She tugged on the reins, and the horse snorted and shied from the competing pressures on the bridle. "Let go of my horse!"

The guard clamped a hand on her ankle. "Go quietly or I'll be forced to arrest you."

"Let go of me!" She kicked at him. Prince Keevan didn't have time to wait until morning. She needed to get past this guard.

"What's going on here?" A voice asked from the darkness. A boy stepped into the light of the guard's torch. He looked to be about sixteen with a mop of dark hair above a round face and square jaw.

Despite his youth, the guard stepped away from Addie and gave the boy a half-bow. "Lord Shadrach, my apologies for disturbing you. I was just escorting these vagrants into town."

Lord Shadrach...must be one of Lord Henry's sons. Addie had heard he had several children, though she'd never paid much attention to them when Lord Henry had visited Nalgar Castle. She met the boy's eyes. "Please. I must see Lord Henry right away. I can't explain now, but it's important. A matter of life or death."

The boy studied her with dark, brown eyes. He rested a hand on the short sword belted at his side, his slim shoulders squared. With a final nod, he turned to the guard. "I'll take them to my father. I believe she's telling the truth."

The guard's jaw clenched, and he glared at Addie. "Dismount."

She slid from the horse, her knees nearly giving out. She tottered over to Prince Keevan. He was unconscious, his skin hotter than it should have been given the cool, autumn air curling around them.

Lord Shadrach led the way across the lawn. He helped the guard untie Prince Keevan and together they carried him inside and laid him on the floor in the entry of Walden Manor. Addie stared at the grand staircase rising to the second floor. Dark, wood paneling lined the walls while burgundy rugs covered the stone floor. On the wall above the staircase's landing hung a large painting depicting a battle.

"Wait here while I fetch my father." Lord Shadrach hurried down a corridor on the other side of the staircase. Addie shifted from foot to foot, wringing her hands to restore feeling to her fingers. Would Lord Henry take the time to see her?

Scuffing boots drew her attention back to the corridor. A tall man with dark brown hair and beard strode into the candlelight, trailed by Lord Shadrach. The matching square jaw and brown eyes told Addie the older man must be Lord Henry Alistair.

His gaze swiveled from her to Prince Keevan sprawled on the floor. Both eyebrows shot up, his eyes going wide.

Addie couldn't let him ask any questions here, not while others could overhear. Captain Stewart had stressed secrecy above all else. Swallowing and trembling, she stepped forward and hurried through a curtsy when Lord Henry's mouth began to open. She forced herself to speak before he could. "I'll explain, but not here, sir. Captain Stewart at Nalgar Castle told me to speak only to you."

Lord Henry studied her, as if trying to figure out what a scullery maid in a dingy dress was doing in Walden Manor's entry hall with the wounded prince. Addie wrapped her arms over her stomach. In the safe, comfortable world of three days ago, there would've been no explanation.

But Acktar wasn't the same as it had been three days ago. Even if no one even knew it yet.

Apparently Lord Henry couldn't think of a reasonable explanation because the wrinkles remained on his forehead when he turned to the guard. "Take her horse to the stable and return to your post."

The guard nodded, his mouth pinched, and scurried out

the door. As soon as the door clacked shut behind him, Lord Henry hurried to Prince Keevan's side. "Shad, fetch the healer. Miss, can you help me get him upstairs?"

After heaving him into the saddle that morning by herself, carrying him up the stairs should be no problem. Addie grabbed Prince Keevan's legs while Lord Henry lifted his shoulders. They maneuvered up the broad staircase. Addie's palms grew slick, but she dug her fingers into the prince's boots. She refused to drop him. She'd grown up scrubbing pots and hauling water. Surely she could haul the prince up one flight of stairs.

They reached the top and shuffled along the upstairs corridor to a room all the way at the end of the hallway. Lord Henry managed to open the door, and they hauled the prince inside. In the dark, Addie got an impression of a bed, a thick rug, and one tiny window set in the far wall.

She dropped the prince's legs on the bed just as footsteps pounded in the hall. Lord Shadrach burst into the room, an old man huffing at his heels. The man carried a leather satchel while his grey hair spiked around his head. Lord Henry lit the lamp and several candles while the healer set his bag on the bedside table.

When the healer turned to the prince, he started and shot a glance at Lord Henry.

Lord Henry gave a slow nod. "I know. I don't know what happened yet, but you'll understand why this has to be kept in absolute secrecy."

"You have my word." The healer returned his own, slow nod.

Addie didn't know how the healer had recognized Prince Keevan so quickly. Had the healer worked at Nalgar Castle?

Or had the royal family visited Walden Manor enough for the healer to recognize him?

Though, based on his glances between his father and the healer, Lord Shadrach hadn't figured out what was going on, so it probably wasn't the latter explanation. Not that it really mattered. Lord Henry seemed to trust this healer, so Addie had to as well. Now that she'd reached Walden Manor, her task was done. All she had to do now was report to Lord Henry and leave everything in his hands.

While the healer laid out his supplies, Lord Henry clapped his son on the shoulder. "Stay here and assist the healer. Don't let anyone else enter this room."

As Lord Shadrach moved closer to the healer, Lord Henry beckoned for Addie to follow him. Her stomach squiggling into knots, she trailed him from the room and down the stairs. If only Captain Stewart was here to explain. He seemed to know what was going on much better than she did.

Lord Henry led her into what looked like his study. Bookshelves lined the walls while an alcove window seat curved under a bank of windows, the drapes drawn back. The desk stood off to the side under a map of Acktar that covered a large portion of that wall.

Lord Henry slid into the seat behind his desk and motioned her to take a seat in one of the brown, leather chairs placed in front of the oak desk.

Addie perched on the edge of one, ready to jump to her feet if she had to. She'd never sat in the presence of a lord before. She was a scullery maid. But right now, her feet ached too much to refuse the chair he'd offered.

He steepled his fingers. "Would you care to explain what happened to Prince Keevan and how you ended up here?"

How could she explain? There seemed to be so much. Too much blood. Too much death. Too many screams. Should she start with the king's death and get that over with? Or start at the beginning as she'd discovered everything?

"I..." She ran her tongue over her lips. "Two nights ago, I was working late and was going through the royal family's wing when I saw movement. I hid in a linen closet and watched while four boys dressed in black crept down the hallway and...and..."

She curled her fingers into the chair's seat, the leather squeaking. She saw again the blood. Thirteen-year-old Prince Duncan's mutilated body.

"You're safe here." Lord Henry's voice was soft.

But he didn't understand. None of them were safe. Not anymore. And Addie's family was still at Nalgar with those killers.

Addie blinked, and something hot trickled down her cheek. "They killed them, sir. The boys in black killed the princes except Prince Keevan. I found him, hurt and choking, and I tried to stop the bleeding. Captain Uriah Stewart and six of his men found us like that. They got us out and told me to ride here, that this was the only town he could trust besides Stetterly."

Lord Henry sat bolt upright now, his steepled fingers frozen a few inches above his mouth. "The king? Is he still alive?"

"No. I never saw his body, but one of Captain Stewart's men did. He said...he said Lord Respen Felix was parading the king's body around the courtyard."

Lord Henry's hands clenched into fists. "Lord Respen Felix is behind all this? What does he want?"

"I don't know." Her words were shakier, more a wail than words. The horrors of that night, ignored during her desperate ride to Walden, shook through her limbs and down her back. "I don't know what he wants. I don't know what is going on. Captain Stewart said all the generals were dead, and then we went through the guest apartments, and there were women crying and bodies, and I think some of the nobles were killed also, and I just don't know."

"All the generals are dead? Were they sure? Even General Hannoran?" Lord Henry went rigid, his hands sinking into white-knuckled fists on the desk. "And my father? Lord Farley Alistair. Did you see him? Is he alive?"

"I don't know. I'm sorry, but I don't know." Addie shook. She was crumbling. "Captain Stewart stayed behind to help get people out, and I'm sure he'll send a message as soon as he can. But that night, it was chaos. No one knew what was happening."

Lord Henry rested his head in his hands. She couldn't blame him for the silence, for the slump to his shoulders. She'd just told him their world had fallen apart in a night. They didn't even know the full scale or cost yet.

"There is one thing. I think Captain Stewart faked Prince Keevan's death. At least, he tried to. I don't know if it succeeded. He had his men bring in another body as we were smuggling Prince Keevan out."

Lord Henry sighed and scrubbed his face. "So it's possible Lord Felix doesn't know Prince Keevan survived. Thus your secrecy when coming here."

"Yes." Addie flexed her fingers against the leather seat.

That was their reality now. The faint hope that this Lord Respen Felix might not know Prince Keevan was alive. A prince who couldn't talk and might even be dying for all Addie knew about healing.

Lord Henry rubbed his hands across his beard. Lines etched into his face, as if her words had added years' worth of burdens. "Forgive me. I've forgotten my manners. What's your name?"

"Addie. Well, Adelaide Croft." She swung her legs under the chair. He was apologizing to her? When she'd just delivered such news?

The hint of a smile carved into his face. "Addie, I wish to thank you. Your actions saved Prince Keevan's life, and may have saved this country. Acktar owes you a great debt."

Her face heating, she stared down at her swinging feet. "It wasn't anything. Not really. Anyone would've done the same thing in my place. I couldn't have done anything else."

"You could've stayed in that closet in case those assassins came back. But, you didn't." Lord Henry's tone softened. "And, I fear, I must ask you for yet another favor."

"Of course, sir." She was a scullery maid. She wasn't in any position to say no to a lord's request. Yet, she got the feeling that Lord Henry was one of the few lords whose request she was free to refuse.

"As of right now, only you, the healer, and I know Prince Keevan is here. Shadrach knows he is someone important, but he won't ask questions or say anything. Prince Keevan will need tending, and someone has to bring him his meals. The healer can only come and go so much, and I can't ask one of the servants and add yet another person to those who already know." Lord Henry leaned his elbows on the table, his eyes soft. "I am sorry to ask more of you, but would you be willing to be his nurse? Nothing more than bringing him his food and switching the bandage."

Addie swallowed. Partly from nerves, but partly because she knew she could say no, and Lord Henry wouldn't force her. If she wanted, she could walk away now.

But she was a scullery maid. She wasn't the type to sit around at ease when there was work to be done. Her mama raised her better than that.

Besides, this was her prince. How could she refuse to help him when he had just lost his entire family?

"It...It would be my honor, sir."

With that Addie linked her future to the prince. For how long? How long would this nightmare drag on?

When Keevan woke, he blinked at the unfamiliar ceiling above him. He remembered hard ground, prairie grass, and cold night wrapped around him. Now four green-painted walls enclosed him with only a tiny window to let in the daylight, no furniture besides the bed, a small table, and a chair. A single green rug covered the wooden floor and matched the green coverlet of the bed. He ran his fingers over the blankets piled over him. Good quality.

Was this Walden? He had no memory of reaching it.

He touched his face and traced the line of bandages. Someone had done a more professional job than that girl's haphazard attempts.

The girl. He glanced around the room, but it was vacant except for himself. Surely Lord Henry was treating her well enough. She deserved some sort of compensation for all her efforts. She had saved his life, even if she was an unrefined scullery maid.

The door creaked open. But instead of the girl, Lord Henry strode inside, his face lined. When his gaze swung to Keevan, he didn't smile. He slid into the chair and rested his elbows on his knees.

Keevan opened his mouth and tried to make a sound. Any sound. But nothing came out but a wheeze. He fisted his fingers into the blanket. He couldn't even ask any of his questions. He was helpless. Voiceless.

"Don't try to talk." Lord Henry scrubbed a hand along his beard. "The healer said you shouldn't try to talk for a few weeks."

Keevan relaxed into the pillow. Only a few weeks of silence. He could handle that, right? It couldn't be that bad, especially not after...

But he couldn't let him think about that. He couldn't let his thoughts go anywhere near that numb part of his heart. The part that belonged to his family.

Lord Henry sighed. "You should be able to talk again, but it could be months. And the healer isn't sure what kind of lasting damage this wound might have caused."

The numbness spread deeper into Keevan's chest. Months? Should? What if he never regained his voice?

He couldn't think about it. He simply had to.

Lord Henry rested a hand on Keevan's shoulder. "I've written to your Uncle Laurence and Aunt Annita. I couldn't tell them you had survived, but I requested they come here as quickly as possible."

Keevan swallowed and turned his face away. If he

could've asked about his family, he wasn't sure he would've. Did he want to know for sure what had happened to them? Or would it be better to go on wondering and cling to a shred of hope?

"I'm sorry, Your Highness. Your family..."

Keevan squeezed his eyes shut. He didn't want to hear Lord Henry's next words. His father and mother. Aengus. Rorin. Little Duncan. Not all of them. Please, not all of them.

"None of them survived."

Pain tore through Keevan's chest. No. Please no.

How could he be the only one left? Why, of his whole family, would he survive? The least of them. The worst of them. Aengus, at least, had been training to rule. Rorin acted so old and mature even at fifteen. And Duncan. How could anyone have leaned over him and slit his throat? He was only thirteen. Too young to die like that. Too young to die at all.

Lord Henry's hand tightened on Keevan's shoulder. "I'm sure God must have a purpose in sparing your life."

Keevan's jaw tightened. A purpose. What kind of purpose would include a thirteen-year-old boy's death? What kind of plan included tragedy such as this?

He couldn't understand. Not any of it.

The only thing he could do was ignore the pain. Shove it into a hard, cold lump in his chest.

He wouldn't cry. He wouldn't feel.

The door creaked, and the girl stepped inside. She stopped short, her eyes darting between Lord Henry and Keevan. "He's awake! I mean, glad to see you're awake, Your Highness. Do you need something to eat? The healer said you could have some broth. I'll fetch some."

The girl spun on her heels and dashed from the room.

Lord Henry stood. "I'd better return to my duties. You'll be well taken care of in the meantime."

As soon as he left, Keevan fisted his hands and fought the tightness in his throat. His family. Gone.

Why was Keevan the one to survive? Of all his brothers, why him?

Too soon, the girl returned, this time carrying a tray with a steaming bowl on it. She set it on the table next to him and perched on the edge of the chair. "I don't know if you're hungry, but the hot broth might feel good on your throat. At least, my mama's soup always feels good when I have a sore throat. Here, let me help you sit up. Do you think you can feed yourself?"

She wrinkled her nose, one hand on his pillow, the other tugging on his arm. Keevan shifted and did his best to sit up at her prompting. His head spun, and pain shot down his neck.

When he was propped up against the pillow, the girl held the bowl out to him. He tried to look down to see it, but the bandages around his face and neck prevented that much movement. His wound throbbed with renewed agony.

She yanked the bowl away from him so fast some of the broth sloshed onto her fingers. "Guess I'll have to feed you. Sorry, Your Highness."

He gritted his teeth. How many more indignities would he have to suffer?

Blinking, Keevan had to turn away from the girl for a moment. Who was he to complain about a few indignities—even the loss of his voice—when his whole family lay dead?

The girl dipped a spoon into the broth, blew on it, and

held it out to him. He forced himself to allow her to shove the spoon into his mouth. This girl was feeding him like a mother fed a child. Like his mother must've once fed him when he was a toddler.

He squeezed his eyes shut. He'd never feel his mother's touch again. Never see her soft smile when she tried to keep the peace between Keevan and his siblings to prevent bothering their father.

"Think you can manage another bite?"

He faced the girl again. Her eyes were large and brown, set in a round face framed with spirals of brown hair puffing out from her attempts to tie it back. After all this time, he still didn't know her name.

He submitted to several more mouthfuls before the pain in his throat grew too great to swallow another bite.

After she helped him settle back into the covers, she gathered the dishes and started for the door. Pausing, she turned back to him. "Is there anything I can get for you?"

His voice back. His country back. His home back.

But those things were out of her power.

And answering her question out loud was out of his.

Keevan held his left hand flat and made writing motions with his right hand.

Her forehead puckered as she stared at him. "You want to...paint your hand?"

He heaved a sigh, then winced when the hiss of air tore through his throat. Surely the infuriating girl wasn't that dense. He tried again.

She stared several more minutes until her eyes and mouth widened. "Writing! You're writing! You want stuff to write with."

Yes. He nodded as much as he could past the pain and the bandage.

"I'll be back as soon as I can with ink and paper."

This time when she returned with paper, ink, and a bowl of steaming water, he drew his knees up and balanced the stack of papers where he could see them. She helped him position the ink so that he wouldn't spill anything.

Writing the one question he'd been burning to ask for two days was like the first breath of spring warming the castle stones. He still couldn't talk, but he could *communicate*. He could be more than the silent, almost corpse that green-eyed assassin had turned him into.

What is your name?

He held the paper up to her. She squinted, probably trying to decipher his handwriting. It had always been a little less than perfect even without the messiness added from trying to write on his knees without moving his head.

She turned from the paper to him and dipped into a small curtsey. "I'm Adelaide Croft, Your Highness, but most people just call me Addie…" She trailed off, as if realizing he wouldn't be calling her anything out loud.

This was progress. Hopefully, the words under his pen would be enough noise to banish the silence in his head, the pain in his chest. His family was dead, and he didn't know why. He didn't even know what had become of their bodies.

Addie opened the one drawer in the bedside table, revealing layers of bandages and other medical supplies. "I'm supposed to change the bandage right about now. Sorry, Your Highness. You were still unconscious last time when the healer showed me how to do it properly, and…well, I'm a scullery maid. I'm still learning, all right?"

He gritted his teeth. In other words, she would probably bumble through this. Why couldn't the healer change the bandages? They wouldn't risk Keevan's health by giving his care over to someone totally incompetent, would they?

But like everything since that knife had flashed down, he was helpless to protest. *Go ahead.*

She unwrapped the bandages from around his face and neck. He tried not to look at her as she bent over him. Not only was it awkward, but she also seemed unaware of the view some of her movements gave him.

But that was his problem. She was his nurse, and it was his problem to keep his thoughts and eyes where they belonged.

Once she'd divested him of the bandages, she grasped his chin and turned his face toward her to get a better look at his face. What did the wound look like? A gaping, mangled line of flesh tracing along his cheek and down to the base of his throat. He couldn't see it himself. If he wanted, he could ask for a mirror.

He didn't. He'd rather not know.

But at least the girl seemed in better control of her stomach this time, even if her face had paled.

When she dabbed the gash with a warm, wet rag, he clenched his fingers and squeezed his eyes shut. A hiss of air escaped him. It would've been a whimper, or a groan, if he could've managed it.

The pain changed. A hand was on his throat. A green-eyed assassin leaned over him, a knife flashing in the moonlight. Pain coursed through him, stealing his strength, stealing his voice. He couldn't even cry out.

He lashed out, trying to stop the knife from coming down this time.

Someone yelped. A high-pitched sound, at odds with the darkness and moonlight swirling across his vision.

He forced his eyes open and found himself staring at Addie, her wide brown eyes framed by her mass of curls. He followed her gaze to see his fingers wrapped around her wrist, squeezing tightly.

What had he done?

He released her wrist. She snatched her hand back, but not before he caught a glimpse of the red marks his fingers had left in her skin.

He'd hurt her. He gulped in ragged breaths, each one tearing through his throat like more knives threatening to finish what that assassin had started. Keevan had tried to be better. Tried never to see fear and hurt and tears form in a girl's eyes because of him again.

But he wasn't better. He was still the same.

Why had he been the one to live? Of all his brothers, why had he been the one spared when any of his brothers would've been more worthy of life than him?

He should reach for the pen and paper to tell her he was sorry, but somehow, dashing off those two words seemed too trite for what he wanted to tell her.

"I'm sorry, Your Highness."

He whipped his head back to her, flinching at the pain that action caused.

She rubbed at her wrist, then paused. "I should've realized you might not react well to having someone touch your neck. After what happened, it's probably expected."

Now he did reach for the pen and ink. *I'm so sorry.*

"You didn't realize it was me, did you? You were remembering that assassin." She reached for the jar of salve again.

He shook his head. A year ago, he might've accepted the excuse. Yes, he had been remembering the assassin and the memory had taken over. But, he'd still hurt her, and that wasn't all right. Could never be all right.

Wriggling his hands under the blanket, he tangled the fabric in his fingers, the best he could do at tying himself down. When he was ready, he met Addie's eyes and gave her as much of a nod as he could manage.

Pursing her lips, she set to work spreading the salve across his wound again. This time, he didn't close his eyes, and he didn't look away from her. As long as he focused on her brown eyes, the memory only lurked in the dark shadows of his mind.

Yet another thing the green-eyed assassin had stolen from Keevan. His sanity.

And someday, that assassin would pay for it.

5

Addie headed for the back kitchen door. Another group of refugees had come from Nalgar. Her parents and siblings had yet to arrive, but maybe they would with this group. Or maybe the next one. Or the next...

Or maybe they'd never come at all. Maybe those Blades would target them for some reason or they wouldn't be able to get out or Lord Felix—King Respen as he was calling himself—would start arresting Christians at Nalgar like Lord Beregern was doing at Mountainwood.

She nodded at the somber cooks and scullery maids as she eased through the kitchens. No one smiled at Walden right now. Not when their lord and his family mourned the murders of both the late Lord Farley Alistair and General Hannoran, Lady Eve Alistair's father.

Addie drew in a deep breath and pushed open the door. She slipped past the small kitchen garden and the extensive flower garden filling the back L-shaped part of Walden

Manor. The group from Nalgar gathered in front of the main door. Lord Alistair stood among them, listening to their stories and the information they brought.

Still holding that deep breath, Addie rounded the edge of the flower garden. Surely today was the day she'd spot her papa's mess of curly hair or her brothers' tall figures.

Then, she was staring at it. A shock of curls above broad shoulders. Papa stood with his back to her, his arm tucked against Mama's lower back. Addie's youngest sister Juliana snuggled next to their mother while Addie's four brothers—Frank, Patrick, Brennen, and Samuel—stood in a semi-circle, most with their arms crossed. Frank rested his hands on their sister Penelope's shoulders.

They had never looked so wonderful.

Addie dashed forward and threw herself into the circle of her family. Somehow, one arm ended up around Mama, the other squeezed Samuel. She couldn't even speak, not even when her family jumped, started, stared, and nearly fell over with her weight.

They were safe. They were all safe and together and free from Nalgar.

"Addie." The whisper was so choked she couldn't tell which of her family had said it.

Then they were all around her, hugging, crushing, squeezing, talking, all at once.

Wresting Addie away from Samuel, Mama squeezed her tightly, crushing her against her soft, ample frame. "I was so worried about you. Captain Stewart would only tell us you had seen something you shouldn't have, but you were safe."

"I'm sorry you were so worried." Addie squeezed Mama tighter as if that action could banish the lingering taste of her fear from her mouth. Even now, she couldn't tell her family why she'd had to leave or about her new duties caring for Prince Keevan. "I worried about all of you, still stuck at Nalgar with those Blades."

Mama pulled back. "We were fine."

Something hard, like the cast iron of the cook pots, glinted in Mama's eyes and sliced through her voice. It was the same sort of voice she had used when scolding them for a particularly bad misbehavior, yet darker, harder.

Addie suppressed a shiver and glanced at her family. What had happened to them after she'd left?

Juliana grinned, though something in her eyes remained shadowed. "Mama made the Blades sick."

"What?" Addie gaped between her mama and youngest sister.

Samuel smirked until his freckled nose wrinkled. "She put raw meat in their food. They were puking for hours, and some were sick for a few days."

Penelope sighed and grimaced. "It was an awful, stinking mess, though. They didn't know who'd done it, but they had Mama and a few of us maids clean it up. Not fun at all."

Mama shrugged. "It kept them occupied while Captain Stewart sneaked most of the soldiers loyal to the Eirdons out of Nalgar before they could be executed. Lord Felix was furious."

Something in Mama's tone told Addie that someone had paid for that stunt. Probably with their life.

"And then, Papa was asked to carve this crossed daggers symbol into the doors in the dungeon tower—the Blades have taken it over—and Papa made sure he did it really loudly at odd hours of the morning when all the Blades were still trying to recover." Samuel added.

Addie glanced at Papa. He stood with his feet braced a foot apart, his shoulders straight. When he caught her looking, he gave a nod and a smile. Still, something in his stance, the tightness to his eyes and mouth, stabbed at her chest. She never would've recognized it if she hadn't seen it so many times on Prince Keevan's face.

Pain.

What had Lord Felix done to her papa as punishment? She shot a glance at Frank, Papa's apprentice. He looked away. Whatever had happened, Frank, Patrick, and Brennen knew, but the other siblings didn't.

That's what these past weeks had done to all of them. It gave them secrets.

Still, her family had been...brave. Much braver than she'd been.

Lord Alistair strolled in their direction. When he reached them, he held out his hand to Papa. "Welcome to Walden. You must be Addie's father. While I can't tell you all the details, you have every reason to be proud of your daughter."

Papa met her gaze. "I know."

Warmth settled into her chest and fingers. Her papa was proud of her. She'd always known it, but hearing him say it out loud in front of all her brothers, sisters, Mama, and Lord Alistair meant something more. Especially after what they'd all been through.

Lord Alistair waved toward the manor. "I'll have a set of rooms readied for all of you. Come with me, and my wife will show you to where you can rest and clean up after your journey."

Addie's papa and mama fell into step behind him, though they cast glances at Addie, as if wondering what she'd done to merit the lord and lady of Walden personally seeing to their needs and giving them rooms in the manor house itself while most of the refugees were being housed in the town or guard barracks.

Addie hung back. She couldn't explain. She'd helped save Prince Keevan's life, and now she was one of the few who knew he was alive. And that placed her family in danger if Lord Felix ever suspected anything.

As he moved to walk past, Addie grabbed Frank's arm. "What really happened at Nalgar? I'm not like Samuel and Juliana. You don't have to shield me from the truth."

Frank glanced between her and their parents' retreating forms, their siblings trailing behind them. He lowered his voice. "He was beaten and whipped. I would've been too, except that Papa told them I was a stablehand like Patrick and Brennen, not his apprentice. Mama and the other cooks weren't able to get their hands on poison, but they tried to make Lord Felix, his Blades, and as many of his soldiers as possible get sick. The head cook and two of the scullery maids were executed for it. Mama might have too, if she hadn't volunteered to see to the mess in the Tower."

Beatings. Whippings. Random executions. Stuff like that happened in other countries. Not Acktar. Not her home.

He wrapped an arm around her shoulders and gave her yet another hug. "It was bad that night, not knowing where you were. Mama and Papa were in a panic. I offered to look for you, but there was too much chaos and fighting. It was hours before Captain Stewart told us you were safe."

"I'm sorry." Addie wrapped her arms around her brother's strong, solid waist. She couldn't change the events of that night. Even if she could go back, she wouldn't do anything differently. Prince Keevan's life would still be more important than letting her family know she was safe.

Frank pulled away, though he kept his arm resting on her shoulders. "We'd better catch up with the others. Mama hasn't let any of us out of her sight in over a week."

As they turned toward the manor's front doors, Addie spotted a group of riders cresting the southern hill. A banner streamed over their heads. It took her a moment to pick out the black upright sword against a white background.

Lord Laurence Faythe had arrived.

KEEVAN DIDN'T BOTHER OPENING HIS EYES WHEN HE WOKE from yet another nap. There never seemed a reason to. Confined to bed and this room, he was trapped inside four blank walls and silence. So much silence.

He'd tried reading, but the silent words did nothing to fill the emptiness inside him.

Even the tiny window offered a view of little besides the eaves and empty prairie.

Only Addie managed to break the silence. She'd spent hours reading out loud to him or talking while he held up his side of the conversation with scribbled words. But he couldn't keep her here forever. She needed space to breathe and think. Last time she'd left—minutes ago or hours, he really didn't know and didn't care—he'd nearly clutched at her like a drowning man reaching for air and sky.

But another girl's tear-streaked face had stopped him. It would be too easy to force Addie to stay, and forcing her to stay here against her wishes was only a step removed from repeating his past.

He'd always let her go, even if the silence and emptiness drove him mad.

Sighing, he peeled his eyes open. Time to face more silence, more boredom.

Except, he wasn't alone. Uncle Laurence slouched in the seat next to the bed, his head in his hands so all Keevan could see was his short-cropped, red-blond hair.

Keevan's chest tightened, sending shafts of cold into his stomach. Would Uncle Laurence be disappointed that Keevan was the one to live? Was he still angry?

He must've made some noise or the bed rustled because Uncle Laurence slowly raised his head. Lines cut across his slim forehead and around his eyes, eyes that held nothing but a deep sorrow. "Keevan. I'm so sorry."

Keevan blinked and turned his face away. The events of the last afternoon he'd seen his uncle flooded through his mind. Uncle Laurence's steely anger. His words warning Keevan's father that the country wouldn't stand to see him let his sons run wild.

A new pain shot through Keevan. Had Keevan helped cause this? With his drinking and flirting and wildness, had he helped cause this insurrection and his family's deaths?

His hand shook as he reached for the ink and paper. *This is all my fault.*

"No, Keevan. No." Uncle Laurence gripped Keevan's

shoulder, his grip just as firm as it had been nearly a year ago. "If anything, it's mine."

Keevan tried to comprehend the expression on Uncle Laurence's face. Guilt. Sorrow. Grief. A deep weariness.

"I knew many in the country were unhappy. I knew your father was struggling to hold everything together. Yet, in my own anger, I withdrew my support right when my king and my brother-in-law needed it most."

Had it only been two weeks ago that Aengus had explained what it had meant for Uncle Laurence to delay showing up to the Gathering of Nobles their father had called? And why Lord Lorraine and a few others had also done the same?

Strange how that delay was the reason Uncle Laurence and the others were alive now.

My father wasn't a good king, was he? Keevan wasn't sure what made him write the question. Did he really want to know the answer?

Uncle Laurence heaved a sigh. His sharply blue eyes focused on Keevan. "Your father would've made a good lord or perhaps a good farmer. But ruling the whole country was too much for him, and, worse, he refused to share the burden. But he did his best. Remember that. No matter what anyone else tells you, your father did his best. It just wasn't enough."

The weight of those words settled onto Keevan's chest. Uncle Laurence and Lord Alistair would expect him to step into his father's place. To reclaim the throne. To become something he never should've been.

But what if it wasn't enough? What if *he* wasn't enough?

There wasn't any *if* about it. He wasn't enough. He was a

failure. And Uncle Laurence knew exactly how much of a failure he was.

"Keevan."

Uncle Laurence's soft, but firm tone drew Keevan to meet his gaze again, as much as the shamed part of him didn't want to.

"We both can learn from our mistakes."

Then, as if to make sure Keevan couldn't miss the meaning of those words, Uncle Laurence hugged him.

Maybe it was the hug, the first he'd gotten since his parents had died. Maybe it was the gentle, choked tone in Uncle Laurence's voice and knowing for the first time in a year Uncle Laurence had forgiven him. Or perhaps, it was seeing Uncle Laurence and knowing he, Aunt Annita, Renna, and Brandi were the only family Keevan had left.

Tears gathered in Keevan's throat, hot and sharp as the green-eyed assassin's knife. He tried to swallow them back. Tried to reclaim the emptiness.

It did no good. Keevan sobbed. Short, hard sobs, noiseless except for a choking whine in his throat.

More arms wrapped around him, and he heard Aunt Annita's voice and felt her touch against his hair. But he couldn't raise his head from Uncle Laurence's shoulder and couldn't stop his keening.

His family was dead. His voice was gone. The country was in shambles. And the weight of all of it rested on Keevan's shoulders.

And just like his father, he would never be enough.

Keevan's room had never been so crowded. It almost made him wish for the silence and emptiness again.

He sat on the bed, legs dangling over the edge. Aunt Annita perched on the bed next to him while Uncle Laurence stood next to her. Across the room, Lady Lorraine sat ramrod straight in the chair, her blond hair braided and coiled about her head. Lord Lorraine paced back and forth, his tall, straight form casting skinny shadows against the wall from the light of the lamps.

Captain Stewart leaned against the wall a few feet away from Lord Lorraine. Lines dragged across the captain's face, as if he hadn't slept the entire two weeks he'd remained behind at Nalgar Castle.

Lord Alistair leaned against the door, probably to feel his son Shadrach's knock to warn them of trouble. With the amount of guards crawling around Walden, it should be the safest place in all of Acktar.

Then again, Nalgar Castle should've been safe, yet those black-clothed Blades had gotten through anyway.

Keevan shifted and tried to pay attention as Lord Lorraine and Lord Alistair debated whether or not Flayin Falls should be added to their list of potential allies.

Keevan should've been the leader here. He should've been stepping up and making a place for himself as the future king. Instead, he was a child staying up past his bedtime. The lords and ladies assembled in this room were perfectly capable of making wise decisions for the country without his help. Keevan had nothing to contribute besides his name and bloodline.

Honestly, they should make Uncle Laurence king and be

done with it. Uncle Laurence and Aunt Annita would make a good king and queen. They would rule fairly and wisely.

It'd be better than placing an inexperienced, worthless boy on the throne.

"Should we tell them Keevan is alive?"

Keevan jerked his head up at Lord Lorraine's question.

Uncle Laurence was already shaking his head. "No, too risky."

"We'll have to tell them something. They won't rally behind a leaderless cause, especially if they don't know an heir to the throne exists." Lord Lorraine paused his pacing long enough to rest a hand on Lady Lorraine's shoulder.

Aunt Annita set aside the pen and paper she'd been using to create the lists of allies and enemies. "You may have forgotten, but I am an Eirdon and I was a princess. It's a little unusual for succession to skip over to a sister, but, somehow, I don't think anyone will argue too much, especially when the alternative is a rebel lord leading a bunch of Blade assassin boys or whatever they're called."

Lord Lorraine shifted, like he had forgotten.

A smirk touched the corner of Aunt Annita's mouth and sparkled in her eyes.

Uncle Laurence glanced at Aunt Annita, and a hint of a smile crossed his face. But the smile faded just as quickly as it had come. "We need a leader. That's what we'll call him. The Leader. The other lords and ladies will assume that leader is me, and, if Respen suspects anything, his attention will also be drawn to me, not Keevan."

At the look Uncle Laurence and Aunt Annita shared, Keevan stifled a shudder. Uncle Laurence was purposefully, knowingly stepping into the center of danger to protect Keevan.

It was too much sacrifice. Keevan shouldn't ask it of them. Not for him. He didn't want a crown on his head, especially not with that kind of cost.

The Leader. It was so fake. He wasn't their leader. Uncle Laurence was.

Lord Alistair stroked his close-cropped beard. "I say we go one step further. Unless we are personally with His Highness, we should never use his name or his title, even among ourselves. Even to us, he will simply be the Leader."

"A wise precaution." Lady Lorraine nodded. "But, I fear we have already drawn too much attention to Walden as it is by meeting here. All it will take is one thorough search of the manor by the Blades, and our Leader's secret will no longer be a secret. The Blades are distracted now rooting out dissent at Nalgar, but it won't be long before the traitor Respen sends them to our towns."

"We can hide him in the Sheered Rock Hills." Lord Alistair turned to Keevan. "I'm sorry it will probably have to be rough accommodations, but it wouldn't be for long. Just long enough for us to gather our allies and reclaim the castle."

"The Blades are almost as likely to stumble across him in a cabin in the Hills as they are in a back servants' room." Aunt Annita huffed as she shook her head. Her long, blond curls bounced across her shoulders.

"Not if he's far enough in the Sheered Rock Hills." Lord Alistair's mouth twitched as if in a smile. "I believe you have a friend who might know just the place?"

Aunt Annita grinned and tapped the pen on the pad of paper. "Ah, yes. He would know, if anyone does."

Uncle Laurence drew in a deep breath. "I'd like to send Renna and Brandi along with Keevan. If Respen's attention is going to be focused on me and Annita, I'd rather Renna and Brandi were far away."

Keevan swallowed, ignoring the ache in his throat. Stuck in a cabin with his cousins? He'd tormented them last time he'd seen them, and a year probably wasn't long enough for them to have forgiven him yet.

"It's decided then. We'll gather our men and allies and reclaim Nalgar Castle." Lord Alistair stated it with so much assurance, Keevan couldn't help but believe it would happen.

And that frightened him as much as reassured him. Once they took back the castle, they would all expect him to wear the crown. To rule.

He wasn't ready. Surely they all had to know it.

Captain Stewart cleared his throat, drawing attention to himself for the first time. "No, it isn't decided. Our prince hasn't given his approval of our plan, yet."

The others in the room jumped and turned to Keevan as if they'd forgotten he was there.

He shifted on the bed, unable to meet their gaze. Why did they need his approval, really? They were the planners. They were the ones who would put this plan into action. What was he besides a figurehead? He wasn't their leader. Not really.

He opened his mouth and tried to get a sound—any sound besides a hiss—but nothing came. All he could do was nod.

Apparently, a nod was good enough.

Captain Stewart crossed the room and knelt in front of

Keevan. He clasped his right hand over his heart and bowed. "Your Highness, I want you to know, I pledge my loyalty to you as the rightful Eirdon heir to the throne. I will fight to my very last breath to restore Acktar to you."

Keevan swallowed. He was so unworthy to be taking pledges like this. He wasn't a king.

When Captain Stewart stood, Lord and Lady Lorraine knelt and also gave their pledge. Lord Alistair did the same, his deep voice resonating in the small room.

Then, Uncle Laurence and Aunt Annita got down on their knees. Uncle Laurence bowed his head. "My king."

Keevan wanted to tell Uncle Laurence that he of all people shouldn't bow to him. But he couldn't. His throat remained paralyzed.

He couldn't lead them. He couldn't be their king.

He shouldn't even be alive.

GATHERING ARMIES TOOK TOO LONG.

The snow came, filling the prairie and clogging the passes in the Sheered Rock Hills. Armies couldn't move. Keevan, Renna, and Brandi couldn't flee.

Everything hushed and held its breath until spring.

6

FIVE MONTHS LATER...

Sitting on his bed, Keevan tried not to watch the movement of Addie's mouth as she read out loud from a book of old folk tales she'd found in Lord Alistair's library.

He tore his gaze away. She was merely a maid. He was a prince. Besides, he owed her too much to risk hurting her.

"Are you listening?" Addie raised both eyebrows and peered over the book at him. She perched on the edge of her chair, her feet tucked beneath it. "If you aren't going to pay attention, then I won't waste my time reading."

Keevan cleared his throat, gathered a breath, and said slowly, "I'm listening. Please continue."

His voice rasped like two pieces of wood scraping against each other. Whatever charm his voice had once had, it was gone forever, bled out through the gash across his face and down his neck.

Addie smiled as if those four words were magnificent accomplishments. Perhaps they were. It had taken months for his throat to heal enough for words. Even now, he couldn't talk long without his voice giving out.

Addie opened her mouth, but before she could continue, a knock sounded on the door. Lord Alistair stepped inside a moment later. "Addie, please leave us."

Brow furrowing, Addie closed the book, stood, and slipped past Lord Alistair, shutting the door behind her.

Lord Alistair turned to Keevan, and as soon as Keevan saw Lord Alistair's face, he knew.

His breath seized in his throat. His fingers froze into icicles.

Lord Alistair sank into the chair, a piece of paper gripped in his hand. Red rimmed his eyes. "Keevan, I have...I have received word that your Uncle Laurence..." Lord Alistair's voice choked off. He bowed his head, but not before something wet and shining trickled down his cheek.

No. Keevan took the paper from Lord Alistair. The words blurred, but Keevan could make out enough.

Uncle Laurence. Aunt Annita.

Dead.

Renna and Brandi in hiding.

Keevan's fingers shook. *...one, a small, green-eyed boy, attacked the guards...*

The green-eyed assassin. He was behind this.

Pain hardened in Keevan's chest. Someday, he would track down this Blade that had destroyed his family. He'd track down them all. Any boy who could look down into Duncan's face, see Uncle Laurence's longsuffering expression, or witness Aunt Annita's smile and still bring the knife down deserved to suffer.

Keevan wasn't a leader yet. But he would become one if that was what it took to wrest Acktar away from these killers.

"I will not leave Renna and Brandi in danger." Lord Alistair whirled. "Laurence..." His voice broke, and he had to clear his throat to continue. "Laurence wanted to send them to safety with Prince Keevan. I can't disregard their wishes."

Keevan gripped the edge of his bed. No one seemed to doubt that he would have to leave. He had no choice.

"I'm not happy with this either, but an Eirdon has to stay in Acktar if we are ever going to rally the rest of the towns to our cause." Lord Lorraine crossed his arms. "To keep Prince Keevan safe, Renna and Brandi have to stay."

"I'm sorry, Henry, but it's a risk we all are going to have to take. You agree that our best policy at the moment is to lure Respen into believing he has won?" Lady Lorraine quirked an eyebrow.

It wouldn't be hard. Keevan tightened his grip on the blankets beneath him. By all appearances, Respen *had* won.

"Yes." Lord Alistair slumped against the door.

"That means none of us can flee because as soon as we do, Respen will know we have a place to run to and he will send his Blades to find it." Lord Lorraine rested his hand on Lady Lorraine's shoulder and squeezed. "We can't send our wives and children to safety. Not my Jolene. Not even your baby Esther. I know it sounds harsh to leave the ladies

Rennelda and Brandiline in danger, but it's the same danger we all share."

A danger Keevan was fleeing. Like a coward.

But what could he do? Lord Alistair and Lord Lorraine had agreed it was necessary. Keevan couldn't stay here. It was only a matter of time before one of Respen's Blades searched Walden Manor, and if they stumbled across Keevan, they'd finish what that green-eyed Blade started.

"We're planning a long war now. We have to play for time." Lady Lorraine smoothed her skirt. "We have to look vulnerable, all the while sending men and supplies to a hidden base where we can train and prepare. We'll have to be patient."

Addie spread her fingers toward one of the fires dotting the meadow, though she wasn't cold. Even though the early spring air nipped at her nose and back, she huddled next to her sisters, keeping warm with their body heat. Her family arranged in a circle on the other logs, Mama sharing a log with Papa, Frank with Samuel, while Patrick and Brennen perched as far apart as they could on another.

She let her eyes drift to the other campfires. There were about fifty of them making this first journey into the Sheered Rock Hills to carve out a hidden base somewhere only their guide Walter Esroy knew. Most were soldiers from Nalgar Castle and their families. Captain Stewart's wife, son, and daughter, sat beside one of the nearby fires, though Captain

Stewart had yet to arrive. Next to them, Walden's healer, his wife, and his children with their families crowded the rest of the circle. Besides Addie, the healer was the only one in this entire meadow who knew that when Captain Stewart returned, he would have Prince Keevan with him.

"Do you want your last piece, or can I have it, Addie?" Samuel was already reaching for the strip of meat hanging from a stick over the fire.

"Go ahead." Addie barely finished waving before the meat disappeared into her brother's mouth.

So far, her family had yet to ask why they'd been chosen to go along. Lord Alistair had told Papa it was because of his carpentry skills, which would be needed in building cabins. Perhaps a good enough reason on its own, but not the only one.

No, the real reason they were a part of this group—near the top of the list Lord Alistair had shared with Prince Keevan before burning it—was her.

Anyone besides Lord Alistair and Lord and Lady Lorraine who knew Prince Keevan was alive was being sent with this group, along with their families to make sure Respen would never have a chance to pressure them for information.

Voices came from the treeline. The sentry called a halt; a deeper voice answered.

Talk around the campfires stilled. Both Papa and Frank reached for logs from the stack by the fire. Juliana wrapped her hands around Addie's arm and squeezed.

This was the world they lived in now. One where every stray sound could be an enemy. Had any of them truly relaxed since the night Respen's Blades drenched Nalgar Castle in blood?

Captain Stewart stepped from the line of trees into the orange haze of firelight. His gaze was hard, unflinching, as it swept over them. "I am about to entrust you with our country's greatest secret and hope, but before I can, I must know where each and every one of you stand. Do you stand with the Eirdon line? Will you give your life if necessary to see to it that the traitor Respen Felix doesn't keep the throne he has stolen?"

Addie rubbed her hands together, chills trailing down her arms. Captain Stewart's words held a weight, so heavy that even the soldiers didn't immediately jump up with bravado and shouting. No one did. Instead, a pause hushed the meadow, all except for the faint rumble of the waterfall in the ravine on the far side.

Captain Stewart's wife rose to her feet. Her long, straight brown hair fell past her shoulders, and her expression remained hard as the sword buckled to her husband's side.

A moment later, Captain Stewart's eighteen-year-old son and fifteen-year-old daughter also stood.

Addie didn't pause to think until she was already halfway to her feet. But when her brain caught up with her actions, she forced herself all the way upright, even though fifty pairs of eyes now focused on her. No one else sitting around the fires, except for the healer, knew the depth of what Captain Stewart was asking besides her.

Perhaps that made it easier for her, not harder. No one else knew who they were pledging their lives to protect.

That made it even more amazing when one by one, the

soldiers around the different fires clambered to their feet, their wives and children rising with them.

Papa and Mama were gaping at her as if they couldn't figure out why their daughter had been so eager to pledge her life. Patrick and Brennen shared a grin, and hopped to their feet like it was some kind of game they didn't want to miss.

Frank's eyes had a searching look as he met Addie's gaze and stood. Moments later, the rest of her family joined her on their feet. Soon they would know the reason why.

Captain Stewart gave a sharp nod and waved his hand. A cloaked figure stepped from the treeline, paused, and tossed back his hood. The firelight played along his golden hair and the red-white scar across his cheek and neck.

Six more men stepped from the treeline, and Addie could just make out enough of their faces to recognize the same six soldiers who had helped smuggle Prince Keevan out of Nalgar all those months ago. Of course they would be leaving too. They knew too much, just like she did.

Papa stiffened, and Mama gasped. Their actions mirrored the others in the meadow who had seen the prince enough times at Nalgar Castle to recognize him now.

Frank crossed his arms and raised his eyebrows. "You don't seem surprised, Addie."

She shifted, glancing between her family before focusing on the fire. "I might have kind of sort of saved Prince Keevan's life."

It sounded pretentious when said like that. She hadn't done all that much. Captain Stewart and his men had done the real saving.

Addie glanced toward Prince Keevan as Captain Stewart led him deeper into the meadow. "Well, not all the way. I just staunched the bleeding."

Papa sat down. "I believe it's time we finally heard the real story of what happened that night."

She didn't have to ask which night. None of them did.

Sighing, she reclaimed her seat on the log. It would be an immense relief to finally tell them the whole truth. As she began, her younger siblings all stared at her with wide eyes, almost like she was a hero or something. Her three older brothers exchanged glances, the muscles in their fingers and arms flexing like they intended to take on a Blade to protect her. Papa and Mama somehow managed to look proud and worried at the same time.

A pang shot through Addie's stomach, and for a moment, she had to pause and catch her breath in the telling. What caused that pang? And why did she have the urge to glance toward the fire where Prince Keevan now huddled, surrounded by his guards?

She didn't...*miss* him, did she? Now that the secret was shared, she didn't have to be his caretaker any more. He wasn't locked in a room with only her and Lord Alistair occasionally dropping by for company.

No, he was the prince. Their future king. It was time he became that king.

And she was nothing more than a scullery maid, so beneath his notice he shouldn't even remember her name.

It didn't really matter, did it? It wasn't like she'd ever thought of him as anything more than her prince.

But she had long winter days reading a book out loud to him. Talking about her family. Listening to him struggle to make his throat form a simple question. What was the weather like today? How much snow was outside? How was her family settling into Walden Manor?

Her prince. Her king. Her duty.

That's all he was.

7

Keevan huddled in his cloak next to a fire after their third day of traveling. Rain pattered against the roof of interlocking pine branches two of the soldiers had constructed over his head.

The six soldiers who'd saved him that night were now his personal bodyguards. He probably should get used to having guards march behind and in front of him everywhere he went, ride alongside him on the trail, sleep in a circle around him at night.

Instead, he was trapped. Just as trapped as he had been for five months in the tiny room in Walden Manor.

He might have survived Respen's assassination, but he was sentenced to prison just the same. A prison of guards, windowless walls, and solitude, yes, but also of the crushing weight of a country's worth of expectations.

"...rain will wash out our trail. A blessing, I think." Walter Esroy's voice boomed over their camp. "If any of those Blade vermin come this way, they won't find us. Damp as it is, I hope the rain keeps up."

Keevan shivered and pulled his cloak tighter over his head. A trickle of water wormed its way through the branches and dripped a steady stream onto his back.

In the rest of the camp, the others hunched under their own makeshift shelters. But many of them had laughter. Siblings teased each other. Friends played games or talked. Parents told stories to their children.

But he was alone. His family was dead. And, he'd never had any friends. Aengus had been a friend, and that had always seemed enough growing up.

But now, it wasn't. Aengus was gone. Buried in a grave somewhere in the hills surrounding Nalgar Castle. Captain Stewart had promised, once they reclaimed Nalgar, that he would show Keevan where the captain and his men had buried Keevan's family. Until then, their graves would remain a mystery to prevent Respen from desecrating their resting place.

Even Keevan's distant cousin Theodor was dead, killed while defending Keevan's father and now buried in Keevan's place with the rest of his family.

A burst of laughter drew Keevan's attention to one of the lean-tos. Addie leaned forward to lightly punch her brother's arm, giving Keevan a brief glimpse of the Raiders board on the ground between them. One of her sisters said something and moved a piece.

Keevan swallowed. Alone. No family. No friends. Just bodyguards and expectations he could never fill.

Captain Stewart stepped past the soldiers on guard and

into the shelter. Shaking droplets of water from his cloak, he sat on a log across from Keevan. "How are you holding up?"

Keevan cleared his throat, gathered a breath, and forced the word out. "Fine." The end of the word disappeared into a hiss of air when his throat failed to cooperate.

Captain Stewart studied him and rested his elbows on his knees. "Permission to speak freely?"

If Captain Stewart was asking permission, then he planned to be exceptionally frank. Not that Keevan cared. Truth or lies, they all hurt. Though, perhaps it was best to hear the truth and get it over with. "Go ahead."

Keevan winced. He no longer knew the sound of his own voice. It rasped like some horrible monster clawing its way from his throat, when it worked at all. Most of the time, it was easiest to say as little as possible to hide his shame.

He should be grateful he had at least regained this much. He still had a voice. But perhaps it would've been better to remain mute and helpless rather than sound like a wretch only to be pitied.

What kind of king sounded like this? Kings made grand speeches. They stirred people into action with the charm of their voice.

Keevan's voice only repelled.

"You've had a hard few months, and as much reason as anyone to grieve. But..." Captain Stewart's face hardened, his body braced as if he expected Keevan to lash out after what he was about to say. "The self-pity has to stop. You may grieve, but you have to step up and lead as well."

Keevan blinked and stared out into the rain, now pouring down harder and faster. Self-pity. Captain Stewart was correct about that. But what could Keevan do? "I can't lead."

Captain Stewart's gaze didn't waver. "Can't or aren't ready?"

Was there a difference? He couldn't. It was too much. It was easier to sit here and let others do it for him.

He closed his eyes, remembering the times his father had stared at the stacks of paper in front of him, paralyzed with the demands of the throne. The way he'd delayed making decisions, even the small ones, because even that one small decision had seemed like too much of a burden.

Was Keevan just like his father? The weight of the kingdom was already breaking him, and he didn't even wear the crown yet.

No matter what anyone tells you, he did his best. It just wasn't enough.

Just like his father, Keevan wouldn't be enough. Why even try?

"Look at me." Captain Stewart's voice had a growl to it, a tone of voice he'd never used with Keevan before.

Keevan dragged his head up. Perhaps he should be angry at insubordination or something like that. But, he couldn't. Why quibble over an order when everyone knew Captain Stewart was the leader here. Keevan was just a boy who should obey.

"A good commander works his way up the chain of command, gaining more responsibility when he has mastered the responsibilities he already has." Captain Stewart waved out into the rain. "No one expects you to be king right now. You aren't ready. But the thing is, you have time. Years, probably. Right now, the only people you have to lead are in this camp. That's it."

Keevan found himself shaking his head. Even that was too much. "I don't know how."

"So you learn how. You observe good leaders. You listen to good advice from those you trust. And, yes, you make friends so that you have people who aren't afraid to tell you the truth. You notice the people under you so that you can serve them." Captain Stewart picked up a saddlebag, drew out three books, and handed the first one to Keevan.

Keevan took it. A book of Acktar's laws.

"This teaches you what laws you have to uphold. And this..." Captain Stewart held out the second book. A history of Acktar. "This is where you learn about the triumphs and failures of past kings."

As if Keevan's father wasn't enough of a warning of how to fail at being king.

Captain Stewart held out the third book. "And this one is the most important one of all."

Keevan took it. A Bible.

Over a year ago, he'd held his own Bible after Uncle Laurence's lecture and resolved to be better than he was. Had all of that resolve bled out of him?

He did his best.

What was Keevan's best? Shouldn't he at least try long enough to find out? Perhaps it was his duty to give it his best effort before he declared himself a failure.

Captain Stewart still studied him with dark brown, solemn eyes. "Practice the kind of leader you want to be now, and when the time comes to wear the crown, you'll be ready."

Practice. The way a soldier practiced with his sword before he ever marched into battle. If things had been different, Aengus would've practiced for years at their father's side before his time came to be king. Keevan wouldn't be able to learn from his father, but he could practice leadership now.

He swallowed and forced a full sentence from his throat. "Where should I start?"

"Perhaps you could start by learning their names."

Learn people's names. Keevan could handle that.

Clasping his cloak tighter around his neck, he stood and stepped from the shelter into the rain. The fat drops pounded on the wool, some of it running off, but some sticking around long enough to seep through.

The two soldiers on guard straightened. "Sir?"

"Stay here. Not going far." It would be easier to learn people's names without two guards flanking his every move. Besides, he was safe here, and he wouldn't be going out of their sight.

He made it three steps before he turned back to the guards. "What are your names?"

The soldiers hurriedly re-straightened, their eyes focused above his head. The one on the left saluted first. "Thadius, sir."

"Arlo, sir." The soldier on the right also saluted.

With their leather helmets pulled over their hair and their identical blank expressions, Keevan couldn't see anything to help him remember which was which. But he had to try.

With a final nod at the soldiers, Keevan turned and continued through the rain. The ground squished under his boots, and by the time he reached the shelter where Addie's family hunched, the leather of his boots also squooshed.

Addie and her family shot to their feet. Her father bowed. "Anything we can do for you, sire?"

"No. I'm fine." Keevan cleared his throat. How did a person go about doing this? "Addie..." His voice gave out. What was the shortest way to ask to be introduced? He waved around at her family, hoping she understood.

Addie's eyes widened. "Oh, let me introduce you to my family."

Keevan nodded. After five months of learning to interpret his gestures, she'd caught on quickly.

"This is my Papa and Mama." Addie pointed to each of them as they bowed to Keevan. Addie's father was tall with a thatch of curly hair and the scruff of a beard. Addie's mother stood next to him, about average height, with the kind of well-endowed figure that made her look ready to pounce with a hug at any moment.

Addie waved to a tall, brown-haired man. "This is my oldest brother, Francis, though we call him Frank. He was my father's apprentice. My next oldest brother Patrick." She pointed at another young man with slightly longer, straight brown hair.

Frank bowed, his expression blank, but Patrick grinned while he bowed.

"Brennen is a year older than me." Addie patted this brother's shoulder. He was shorter than the older two brothers, and his lighter brown hair scruffed along his cheeks and chin. Addie's grin widened. "He and Patrick were stablehands at Nalgar."

Keevan nodded to each of them. Shouldn't he remember them? How many times had Addie's brothers saddled his horse for him? Keevan hadn't noticed. Had he really been that blind to those around him?

Notice. That was his first task to become a leader. Well, he was noticing now.

"This is my sister Penelope. She's two years younger than me."

Penelope huffed. "Only a year and a half. It's nice to meet you, sir." She swayed into a graceful curtsy.

That left only two people in the circle. A boy, who looked to be about fifteen or sixteen, and a girl a year or so younger yet. Addie looped her arm over the boy's shoulders. "This nuisance here is my little brother Samuel. And she's Juliana."

"A pleasure to meet all of you." Keevan bowed to each of them in turn. He drew in a deep breath. Would his voice behave long enough for him to put together a sentence? "If there's anything I can do for you, please let me know."

"We're all right. Thank you, sir." Addie's mother gave another half-bow.

Keevan glanced between them. All so stiff.

How should he act around people? Should he be a prince? Or a person? Was there a way to be both?

That's what Captain Stewart was trying to tell him. Make friends. Actually see those around him.

After all these months of hiding and pain, had Keevan forgotten how to even talk to other people? He'd once been able to charm others. Now...now his voice was that of a monster. But did Keevan have to be a monster as well?

Keevan forced a smile and sank onto one of the logs. "I used to play Raiders with my brothers. Would you like to play another game?"

"I'd like to." Addie perched on the log with several inches of space left between them.

Addie's siblings dropped back to their seats on the logs, silent and staring.

"I think we'll have to do teams, unless a few people don't want to play." Addie shot a glance at Keevan. "I guess I'll be a team with you, if you'd like that."

Five months ago, he'd dismissed her as nothing more than a foolish scullery maid. But she'd saved his life. She'd spent hours with him every day when all she'd volunteered to do was bring him meals and change the bandage. She'd coaxed him into his first sounds and words, and she'd grinned when he'd managed to say his first sentence without his voice giving out.

After all that, they were bonded into something more than just servant and prince. What that bond was, he couldn't be sure. Could it be...friendship?

If it was, he'd do his best to figure out how to be a good friend. Maybe in doing so, he'd figure out how to be a good person and a good leader.

Keevan stared upward at the cliffs rising above the forest and surrounding mountains. Gray spires rose above sheer cliffs with towering pines growing along their base.

"Think it'll do?" Walter Esroy reined in his horse.

Captain Stewart craned his neck. "Can we get up there?"

Walter nodded and pointed east. "If we go around that way, there's a trail up to the cliff top."

Keevan nudged his horse to fall in line with Captain Stewart as Walter set out once again, winding through the dense stands of juniper and pine. Boulders jutted through the undergrowth, and sand slid beneath the horses' hooves.

Two columns of red-gray rock guarded either side of a crevice. The clatter of their horses' hooves echoed off the rocks as they rode between the columns.

Before them, the mountaintop opened into a nearly flat, gravel-covered plain. A few canyons branched down the sides, disappearing among a warren of boulders.

"We'll build temporary shelters tonight and start on the cabins tomorrow." Captain Stewart turned on his heel. "This will make a good stronghold, I think."

"Thought it would." Walter patted his horse's neck. "The Rovers I used to be with, they called this place Eagle Heights. Not many know of it now. Most of the younger Rovers don't like to travel this deep into the Hills."

Sheltered by eagle's wings. Keevan had read about fortresses and high towers the night before. A Bible passage written by a king after being on the run from his enemies.

"Eagle Heights it is." Captain Stewart pointed toward one of the canyons. "We'll begin building shelters over there."

Keevan glanced behind him as the rest of the soldiers and their families entered the mountaintop. Addie and her family scrambled onto the slope. Her eyes flicked toward Keevan, and for the briefest moment, their gazes locked.

After nearly six months of looking over their shoulder,

wondering if that day would be the one a Blade invaded Walden, this was safety. Here they could rebuild their lives. And perhaps, Keevan could build himself into a king worth following.

8

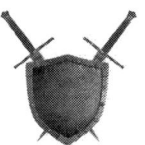

TWO YEARS LATER...

"The latest supplies from Walden arrived."

Keevan glanced up from the stack of papers on his desk in his room in the main cabin. General Stewart strolled through the doorway, the morning sunlight flashing on the streaks of gray in his hair.

Keevan set his pen aside. "Any new families?"

"Five, including several young men who were serving as soldiers for Deadgrass. Their wives and children are with them."

"Make sure the fabric and other supplies are distributed to them first. Give them a section in the lower town by the lake."

"Already done." The lines on General Stewart's face deepened. "Lord Alistair reports he believes Respen has gained a few new Blades."

"How many does that make now?" Keevan rubbed his

thumb along his scar. Once the new families were settled in, he'd have to greet them. His throat would ache by the time he finished talking, but it would be worth it to see the fear leave their faces as they realized they were safe here. "Sixteen?"

"Yes." General Stewart crossed his arms. "They've managed to wipe out the last band of Rovers. They killed them all."

Keevan frowned. The news should've made him happy. After all, the Rovers had troubled Acktar long before Respen and his Blades. But it only added to the hard lump in his chest that never left, no matter how long he lived here at Eagle Heights. "The trade routes will be safer, but it leaves the Blades free to search for us or kill Respen's other targets."

"Walter has already reported increased activity in the Sheered Rock Hills. He believes Respen sent several of his Blades to scout the Hills and the Waste. Looking for a hidden base, perhaps."

"It will take them a while to find us. We're deeper than most ever venture." Keevan pushed away from the table and reached for his sword and sheath leaning against the wall. "Thank you for the report. I'll be practicing if you need me."

"Yes, sir." General Stewart stepped out of the way to let Keevan pass.

Keevan buckled on his sword as he strolled from the main cabin. Addie's three oldest brothers fell into step with him.

Patrick patted his sword's hilt. "Well, sir, you ready to get beat again?"

"I think you're remembering wrong." Keevan returned the grin as they strode down an incline to the flat, graveled area they used as a training ground. To one side, Lieutenant Stewart, General Stewart's son, drilled some of the newest recruits in basic maneuvers. Keevan nodded to them but kept on going until he reached the far side.

Keevan sparred with Addie's brothers for several hours, working his muscles until they burned. When they finished, Keevan swiped his forehead against his sleeve, leaving a wet streak on the fabric. He sank to the ground to rest his aching muscles.

Brennen dropped to the ground next to him. Patrick leaned against a tree on Keevan's other side.

But, it wasn't until Frank crossed his arms that Keevan realized he was surrounded. He tensed and clambered back to his feet.

"I have a deep respect for you, sire, but I have to ask." Frank's jaw flexed. "What are your intentions toward our sister?"

"Addie?" Keevan glanced between the three brothers. "I don't have any intentions toward Addie."

"Are you sure?" Frank's gaze didn't waver. "You and Addie spend a great deal of time together."

"I spend a great deal of time with your whole family. You're my friends. The closest thing I have to family." Keevan's throat closed on the last words. His raised voice rasped hard and painful.

"Then make it clear that friendship is all you desire. Addie is twenty-one. Haven't you noticed the way the other young men in this camp avoid her? They don't dare form an attachment because they think you already have an understanding with her."

"I see." Keevan crossed his own arms, forming a barrier

between him and Frank. What were his intentions toward Addie, really?

Honorable. He would never allow himself to be anything less. Never again.

Could he really ask a girl to love him, knowing he'd once let himself go a step too far? That maybe he would hurt her as he'd once hurt another girl over three years ago?

He wasn't the boy he'd been back then. Time and tragedy had taken away his charm and recklessness. But would he make the same fall if in the same circumstances?

He didn't dare find out. Not with Addie.

For that reason, he could never be more than a friend.

"I have no claim on her." Keevan brushed past Addie's encircling brothers, not sure why the words hurt in his chest even more than they ached in his throat.

But her brothers didn't let him get off that easily. Within a few strides, they'd closed around Keevan once again. He suppressed a sigh. Of course he couldn't run off. Frank, Patrick, and Brennen were his guard detail for the day.

"Why not?" Frank sped up, stepped in front of Keevan, and stopped, arms crossed once again. "Is our sister not good enough for you?"

"What?" Keevan stared at Frank. Behind him, he sensed Patrick and Brennen come to a halt behind him, boxing him in. "No, it's not like that at all."

"Then why not?"

"I'm not good enough for her."

There, he'd said it. The real reason he could never have intentions toward Addie, no matter how much it hurt.

"Don't you think that is up to her?" Frank raised his

eyebrows. "It's her heart to give away, and we think she's given it to you."

Now that was ridiculous. Addie had been distant for months now. She'd even gone back to calling him *sir*. Was that the action of a girl who had given her heart away?

Frank broke his stiff stance to poke Keevan in the chest. "Don't hurt her."

"What do you think I'm trying so hard not to do?" Keevan finally brushed past Frank and kept walking. This time, Addie's three annoying older brothers fell into step a few paces back and didn't try to get in his way again.

Keevan stalked to the main cabin and left Addie's brothers in the entry hall. But even changing clothes and wiping off his sweat with a damp cloth did little to settle his thoughts.

The more he thought about it, the more an ache deepened in his chest. As the prince and heir, he would be expected to marry the daughter of one of the nobles. Maybe even the daughter of a noble who supported Respen to solidify peace after Respen was defeated.

None of the nobles had fled to Eagle Heights yet. And the thought of having to begin courting after taking the throne sometime in a distant, unknown future...that sort of courtship would be all politics.

Was it wrong that Keevan wanted more? Did he even deserve more after the kind of boy he'd been growing up?

But here at Eagle Heights, surrounded by families like the Crofts and Stewarts, Keevan couldn't help but want more. His own parents had loved each other, hadn't they? Keevan couldn't remember seeing otherwise.

Could Keevan move beyond the boy he'd been? Three

years had changed him. He'd lost his family. He'd fled Acktar. He'd begun to be a leader, even if he wasn't yet the king he ought to be.

We both can learn from our mistakes. That's what Uncle Laurence had told him two and a half years ago.

How did Keevan learn from his mistake? Yes, he'd stopped kissing maids in closets. He'd worked to keep his mind from straying where it shouldn't. He'd done his best to treat all women with honor.

But was there more than that? Could he step beyond the flirtations to find what it meant to love a woman as God intended?

Reaching for the Bible General Stewart had given him, Keevan flipped to the first verse Uncle Laurence had had him read all those years ago. Each one still seared into his memory, hot and sharp as his own guilt.

Keevan read, and he prayed, and with his thoughts assembled in his mind, he knew what he had to do.

ADDIE SWEPT THE LAST OF THE DIRT FROM ONE OF THE CABINS reserved for new arrivals. Once the people were settled, they could begin building their own cabin in one of the open places on the mountain or in one of the villages north of the main base of Eagle Heights. Until then, this cabin would be that family's sanctuary.

She peered at her handiwork. Not a speck of dust on the windowsills or floor. The freshly washed curtains filled the space with the scent of sun and mountain breeze. Blankets covered the beds, the mattresses plump with fresh-cut grass.

Others would come with warm food and welcoming smiles, but this was what Addie could do for those fleeing to Eagle Heights. A clean home after the harshness of the trail. Rest after the terror of leaving Acktar with nothing but a few bundles of belongings.

Stepping from the cabin, Addie closed the door behind her and turned toward the next cabin in the row. Her steps halted as her gaze snagged on the huddle of new families.

Keevan stood in the middle of them, smiling and welcoming them to Eagle Heights. Some flinched, probably at the rasp of his voice or the sight of his scar, but others stared, as if they couldn't believe they were seeing a surviving Eirdon heir. Addie's three oldest brothers stood a few feet behind him, hands on swords, eyes scanning for trouble.

Much as she fought the impulse, her gaze latched on Keevan. On the soft tilt of his smile as he asked for each person's name in turn and greeted them personally. The way he bent down and listened intently as the seven children of a widowed woman from Deadgrass gave their names. And, when an old woman tried to bow despite her creaking knees, Keevan gripped her hands and eased her back to her feet, not letting go until he could pass her to her daughter.

Addie should turn away. It did her no good to look and admire. He was her prince. Someday, he would reclaim his throne. And no matter what happened, she would remain nothing more than a scullery maid.

Even if he returned her feelings—which he most certainly didn't—it wouldn't change anything. Would she want to say yes if it meant becoming queen?

It didn't matter. He would never see her as anything

other than his loyal servant, and she could never, ever let him see that she even occasionally daydreamed about something more.

He turned, and for a moment, his gaze snagged with hers. Addie's breath caught in her chest, forming a hard, painful lump.

Tearing herself away, she spun on her heel, gripped her broom, and marched to the next cabin. Scullery maid. That's what she was and always would be.

Barreling inside, she set to work sweeping and dusting with too much energy. Dust flew into the air, and she'd have to redo her efforts once she calmed down. If only it would be as easy to sweep away the flutters from her stomach and the ache in her heart.

Boots scuffed to a halt in the doorway. Addie froze. She knew that rhythm, that silence, because it beat in her head and heart too loudly. Squeezing her eyes shut for a moment, she drew in a deep breath and turned around.

Keevan leaned against the doorjamb, the slanting sunlight highlighting the white scar across his cheek and neck. He remained silent.

"Is there something I can do for you, sir?" Addie gripped the broom handle until the wood cut into her palms. Somehow, her voice stayed steady, even if her heartbeat wasn't. "Your throat probably hurts after all that talking, doesn't it? Would you like me to fetch a hot towel? Or something to drink?"

That's all she was. His servant, his nurse. The one who could tell when he'd strained his weakened throat muscles with too much talking, who knew the best methods to soothe that ache, and one of the few who had guessed his fear of one day losing his voice entirely.

"No, I'm fine." Keevan cleared his throat, a sure sign that he considered his next words important. "Could you please walk with me?"

Did he have something he wanted to discuss with her? Another widow whose home Addie could help clean or an old couple who needed someone to see to their needs? Addie leaned the broom against the wall and dusted off her hands. "All right."

Keevan's far-too-blue eyes swept over her. "It's a request, not an order. If you're too busy, I can come back later."

Did he have to keeping doing things to make her heart race and ache at the same time? It would've been so much easier if he simply gave her orders.

But he always asked. Always made sure she knew she could refuse.

"Now is fine." Might as well get this conversation over with. She'd never be able to get back to work if she knew Keevan wanted to speak with her. It would send her mind into too many scenarios and her heart into too many daydreams.

Somehow, she made it out the door and fell into step a few paces behind him. The respectful distance of a servant to her prince. Actually, it was still too close, but every time Addie tried to put more distance between them, Keevan halted and waited for her to catch up.

Keevan led her from the village and into the trees bordering the lake. He didn't stop until the bustle of people had faded into the soft lapping of water on the pebbled bank and the whisper of pine trees murmuring in the breeze.

Whatever he wanted to talk about must be secret, but why would he take her out here? Why not call her into his study at the main cabin?

This spot, it was almost...romantic. Which wasn't possible. It was probably just convenient.

Keevan cleared his throat again and rubbed at his scar. When he spoke, his face was turned toward the lake. "Addie, are we friends?"

She caught her breath. There was no safe way to answer that. Did he want her to say yes or no? If she said yes, wouldn't that overstep the servant-prince relationship? But if she said no and he'd wanted her to say yes, he'd be hurt.

But weren't they already friends in some way? She'd thought so on the trail all those years ago when Keevan had joined her and her siblings for a game of Raiders, the first of many games over that journey and every winter since. Surely their shared laughter and smiles made them friends.

"Yes." She rubbed her hands over her arms, the callouses on her palms and fingers catching on the fabric of her sleeves.

The rasp in Keevan's voice grew until she could barely pick out his next words. "Do you ever want something more?"

She couldn't answer this question. It wasn't safe for either of them. How did he suspect? What had she done to give herself away?

He had brought her out here to set her straight on how misplaced her feelings were. That's why he'd chosen this private setting rather than call her into his study where everyone would see her enter and leave. At least this way, she'd be able to run off to cry in peace.

What should she say? Should she apologize and promise her feelings would never get in the way of her duties? Or should she lie and tell him she never wanted anything more than friendship and duty?

What would hurt him less to hear?

"No." The lump in her throat turned the lie as raspy as Keevan's voice.

He flinched and sucked in a deep breath. "I see. May I ask why?"

Why did he have to keep interrogating her? Couldn't he just stop and let her get back to her work and her hidden daydreams and leave it at that?

Addie hugged her arms to her stomach. "You're a prince, and I'm a scullery maid. It would be foolish of me to...to entertain notions just because you did me the honor of considering me a friend."

There, that sounded proper and dignified, didn't it? With his face turned away from her, he thankfully couldn't see the blush that heated her face.

"It isn't because of the reputation I had at Nalgar Castle?" He still wouldn't look at her, his body still except for the rise and fall of his shoulders.

"No, I..." Her throat closed. Nalgar Castle, and the fear she'd once felt walking the corridor by the princes' rooms, seemed so long ago. She closed her eyes, remembering the long hours she'd spent in Keevan's room at Walden reading book after book to him to ease his boredom. The times she'd sat across from him, holding a one-sided, nonsense conversation and the aching pauses while she waited for him to struggle through forming a single word to answer her. He'd never done anything to make her fear him then.

Even now, alone in this secluded nook of lake and trees, she couldn't imagine him doing anything worse than this interrogation.

"I had that reputation for a reason, you know." Keevan remained still as the boulders behind him. "One time, I didn't stop when a maid said no. I didn't stop even when she started crying, and I wouldn't have stopped except that Uncle Laurence caught me in time. I didn't even know her name, and the worst part is, that up until the moment he caught me, I didn't care. That's the sort of boy I was, and I pray each and every day I never become again."

She should've been shocked by his confession. But it was as if he was telling her a story about someone else, someone she didn't know. Because she didn't know that Keevan. She only knew the man standing in front of her, the man who would memorize the names of seven children in a family of peasant farmers from Deadgrass just so that he could give each of them a smile.

If she was his friend, then she had to tell him her heart, this part of it at least. Her own gaze latched onto the lake as if its ripples could save her from drowning in this mess of her own heart's choosing. "Whatever boy you were then, he died in Nalgar Castle the night the Blades attacked. You have never treated me anything less than decently. I think...I think someone who has truly repented and prays for God's strength to fight temptation will receive that strength. It is possible to change."

"But what if that change isn't permanent? What if it's still possible to fall back into the same weakness and hurt someone you cared about?"

She shivered and hugged her arms tighter to her stomach. He should ask one of the ministers who'd fled to Eagle Heights over the years. Surely one of them would have a much better answer.

"I think it's time to experience God's forgiveness and let go of your guilt. Hanging onto it and punishing yourself isn't going to atone for anything you might have done in the past. Only Jesus can do that."

The silence dragged on for a minute. Addie tried not to shift. She had to be patient, like she'd been years ago when waiting for him to force his damaged throat muscles to work.

Keevan trailed his thumb over his scar, and his body relaxed, though his face remained turned away from her. "Honestly, I thought you would be a lot more shocked when I told you."

Maybe she would've been a few years ago. But, it wasn't as if the story was a surprise to her. "Well, I'm not. There aren't many secrets among servants at a castle."

"And you still saved me that night?"

"You were hurt. I didn't stop to think too much about it." But now, Keevan had matured into the kind of man she could…Addie couldn't even let herself think the word. Especially not with Keevan leaning against a tree only a few feet away.

He blew out a long breath. "Since my past isn't an issue… what if I wasn't the prince, and we were just Keevan and just Addie…would you want more than just friendship?"

He turned to her then, his eyes searching her face. And Addie found she couldn't lie to him, not when he had opened himself before her like that.

"Yes." The word was nothing more than a whisper, but in the stillness beside the lake, a whisper was loud enough.

Keevan's gaze didn't waver. "And what if I wanted the same?"

She closed her eyes. Would it have been easier if he'd never said it? If they could've gone on as they had been? But now, they had to figure out where they went, and nothing good could come of that. Not between a prince and a scullery maid.

When she forced herself to face him again, he'd come within arm's reach of her, but he didn't touch her. "If I asked to court you, would you say yes?"

She steeled herself. They'd gone too far. They'd been too honest. Both of them were going to be hurt, and the best thing now was to end this. "No. I can't."

"Why not?"

With the rasp to Keevan's voice, Addie couldn't read any emotion in it. Why couldn't he just let this go? Walk away and never speak to her again as anything more than a servant? Couldn't he see this was killing her?

She stepped back, turning to face the lake. "I'm a scullery maid. I can't be anything more than that."

"And I'm just the prince who out of all my brothers lived when I shouldn't have. I can't be king, yet someday I'll have to be if we win this war." Keevan's rasp remained a few feet behind her. "And if that day comes, I'd like to face it with you as my queen."

He couldn't really mean that. This...thing here at Eagle Heights couldn't last once they returned to Acktar. There were rules, and no one, not even a king, was allowed to break them.

She'd run out of room to retreat. The pebbles on the lakeshore squeaked beneath her boots when she gathered her courage to face Keevan again. "Don't you see? I can't be your queen. I'm a scullery maid. My mother was a scullery maid before she worked her way up to assistant cook. My grandmother was a scullery maid. Princes don't marry scullery maids."

"Who's going to argue?" Keevan's mouth quirked as he waved back toward the village. "There aren't any of the nobility here, and the people that are here would be more than happy to see one of their own marry their prince. By the time we return to Acktar, if ever, you would be my princess."

"But...there's politics..." The words sounded faint, even in her own ears. Why was she protesting so much when Keevan was saying more than she'd ever daydreamed about?

She didn't dare let herself hope. It would only hurt all the more when it fell apart.

"I don't want this to be about politics, but if you want to make it that way, then consider this. Acktar changed when the Blades killed my family. Respen has torn this country apart, and if I married the daughter of a noble from either side, the other would see it as favoritism. It would only foster bitterness. But a scullery maid? A marriage clearly out of love and not political? Both sides would just shake their heads."

She was shaking, her eyes blurring so much she could barely make out Keevan's form standing once again within arm's reach. She had to keep denying the way her heart was clamoring for her to give in. This couldn't happen between them. She loved him too much to ever get in the way of his future crown.

He stretched out a hand but still didn't touch her. "May I?"

He'd walk away if she said no. But as much as her mind yelled *no*, her heart lodged in her throat and wouldn't let the word out. Instead, she found herself nodding yes.

Keevan's hand touched her hair, curving her curls through his fingers. "Addie, I don't want you to be more than you are. I want you to be the girl who had enough courage to leave her hiding spot in a Blade-infested castle to see if any of the royal family still lived, who spent months at the bedside of a mute prince smiling and laughing until he finally smiled back, and who cleans cabins without ever expecting recognition for your efforts. You are enough just as you are."

She leaned her cheek into his hand, wishing she was strong enough to drag her heart back to where it belonged. There were certain boundaries a servant and a prince didn't cross, yet he was daring her to cross them with him. And she found herself wanting to defy everything to do it.

"I'm not asking you to rule with me. I want you to serve alongside me." Keevan tipped his head toward her, but he kept several inches of space between them except for his hand caressing her face. "Is there really a difference between a scullery maid and a queen? One serves the castle; the other serves the country."

"Keevan, I..." His name slipped out, and it destroyed the last of her resolve. She leaned her head against his shoulder. "Yes. That's my answer. Yes."

Keevan wrapped his arm around her waist. For a moment, they weren't a scullery maid and a prince. They were just Keevan and just Addie. And it was perfect.

After a moment, Keevan stepped back and eyed her. "I don't know why you even like me. You've given me my smile. You don't flinch when I talk. What have I ever given you?"

What had he given her? Surely she wasn't one of those empty-headed girls who fell for a man's charms and looks without any substance to it?

But Keevan's voice was too harsh to have charm and his scar too gruesome to be handsome.

Perhaps it was the way he saw people. The way he saw her. As if every person here at Eagle Heights was important. As if he knew he carried all their hopes and futures on his shoulders.

It had inspired her to give more than duty required. To see the needs around her and try to help, even when they didn't even know she was helping. For the first time in her life, she'd truly mattered, because of him.

Perhaps she had been looking at it all wrong. There might be a difference between a servant and a king here on earth, but in God's eyes no calling was any better or worse than another. And maybe, just maybe, a scullery maid could be called to be queen someday.

Tipping her face toward him, she finally smiled without having to force it. "You give me a voice."

KEEVAN SAVORED THE FEEL OF HER IN HIS ARMS, SO MUCH more right and sure than anything he'd experienced as a boy. He rubbed his thumb over her chin, stilling when her fingers traced the length of his scar.

Should he kiss her? The look in her deep brown eyes

seemed to be asking him to, but he couldn't be sure. He didn't dare make a mistake, not with Addie.

He leaned closer until only a whisper's breath separated them. "May I?"

Instead of answering, she wrapped her arms around his neck, stood on her tiptoes to close the last fraction of space, and kissed him.

He could've given in. He could've lost himself with the moment.

But, he didn't. The wiser part of him—the part that had spent much of that afternoon in prayer—held him back.

He pulled away from her and discovered there was something highly satisfying in holding onto his self-control instead of giving in to his raging pulse. Her happiness and honor mattered far more to him that any of his own desires.

A voice broke through the haze. "Now that this all is officially settled, I think it's time we went to Mama and Papa's for supper."

Keevan jerked away from Addie, placing a foot of space between them before he turned.

Frank leaned against a tree, his arms crossed yet again. Behind him, Patrick perched on a boulder, flicking pebbles into the lake.

Patrick snapped another pebble, sending it skipping a full four hops before it sank. "Aren't Mama and Papa going to be surprised? Their little Addie courting our prince and someday going to be his queen."

"Frank, Patrick! What are you doing here?" Addie clenched her fists, glaring at her brothers. Red suffused her face from the base of her neck all the way to her hairline.

Frank jabbed a thumb at Keevan. "We're his guard detail. It's our job to know where he is."

"That doesn't mean you had to spy on us!" Addie dipped both hands in the lake and threw the double handful of water at Frank. Most of the water splattered on the ground, but some soaked into the front of his shirt. "And here I was all polite and nice while you were courting Suzanne. The good little sister helping with the wedding and welcoming my new sister-in-law. I should've put burrs in your fancy trousers and watched you squirm through the ceremony."

"Remind me never to get married." Patrick tossed another pebble at the lake.

"Me either."

Keevan spun on his heel, slower this time. Brennen and Samuel stood behind him. Addie's brothers had them surrounded. He sighed and pointed at Samuel. "You aren't even a part of my guard detail."

"Not yet." Samuel grinned, crossed his arms, and looked for all the world like he was trying to match Frank's stance. "I got done with training early today."

Of course he would. Nothing left to do but surrender at this point. Keevan held out his arm to Addie. "I have been craving your mama's venison stew lately. Shall we?"

Addie gripped his arm, glared at her brothers, and dragged Keevan along with her when she marched off.

Her parents weren't surprised to see Keevan. He had dined with them frequently over the years. They weren't even surprised to see Addie glaring at her brothers. What did surprise them was Addie's hand tucked so tightly in Keevan's.

But, Addie's mother gave Keevan a warm hug, and after

supper, her father asked him to go out to the woodworking shed with him.

Keevan had expected it and followed silently. As he stepped into the shed, he gulped a deep breath, the air heavy with sawdust and glue. Without being told, he picked up a piece of sandpaper and scrubbed it over the tabletop where he'd left off the night before.

Addie's father, Garrett Croft, retrieved his own sandpaper and set to work on the other side. For several minutes, neither of them spoke. Keevan relaxed into the rhythm, running his fingers over the silk-smooth surface to search for the tiniest sliver or rough patch.

"Do you love her?" Croft's eyes lifted from the tabletop to Keevan.

"Yes." After so long denying it, the word came surprisingly easy. But perhaps, it wasn't so surprising. Keevan had been slowly, hopelessly falling for her from the moment he lay choking on his own blood and had looked up to see her bending over him, her curls wild and silver in the moonlight.

To this day, her hand was the only one he could stand on his neck. He broke into a sweat whenever the healer poked and inspected as he did several times a year to make sure Keevan wasn't in danger of losing his voice again. But Addie? He never flinched away from her.

He cleared his aching throat. Soon, Keevan's rasp would deepen and hiss in his throat as the weak muscle gave out completely.

"Good." Croft refocused on the tabletop once again.

That wasn't the end of the conversation. By the time Keevan and Croft returned to the cabin, Keevan's voice had given out, and he was content to sprawl on the cabin floor, a damp, hot cloth draped around his neck, while Addie and her family talked and laughed around him.

Her family. And, someday, his family. Four brothers, two sisters, and parents.

He still missed his own brothers and parents, but the ache was less than it had been. He had been blessed with this family instead, a family he never would've noticed had Respen not changed his life so drastically.

If Respen wasn't a murderer and if Acktar's citizens weren't dying under his ax and his Blades' knives, Keevan might have been tempted to daydream about staying lost. About never returning to Acktar and simply living like this forever. A homey cabin deep in the mountains. The smell of glue on his clothes and sawdust under his fingernails. Laughter and smiles unhampered with politics and burdens.

But that's all it was. A daydream. Someday all this would end and Keevan would have to return to Acktar.

Still, he couldn't help but pray it wasn't anytime soon.

9

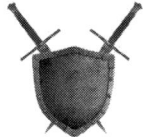

TWO YEARS LATER...

Keevan brushed the layer of sawdust from the cradle. He smoothed his fingers over every inch of it, seeking even the smallest sliver. He couldn't find any.

Papa glanced at him. "Looks about ready to varnish."

That was Keevan's estimation too, but it was good to hear Papa agree. Keevan traced his fingers over the pattern carved into the headboard. "I think I'd better go over this part again. Feels a bit rough here."

Papa nodded, but Keevan wasn't sure it was agreement or simply an acknowledgment. "You did a good job."

Keevan ducked to hide his grin. This wasn't the first piece of furniture he'd built, but, somehow, it felt the most important. In a number of months, his and Addie's child would sleep in here. His son or daughter.

Stomping boots announced a visitor before a soldier

ducked into the shed. He gave a half bow to Keevan. "General Stewart says there's a message from Walden."

"I'll be right there." Keevan set the cradle on one of the workbenches along the side of the shed. Brushing off his hands and grabbing his cloak, Keevan left the shed and headed for the main cabin at the edge of the broad, graveled clearing at the top of the mountain.

Patches of slush still piled against cabin walls and in the canyons. Down in Acktar, the snow was probably gone and planting begun, but up here, mud and slush still ruled.

Scraping off mud from his boots on the front step, Keevan strode into the warm darkness of the cabin's entry hall. Light shone from the meeting room to his left, and he followed the light into the broad space.

General Stewart sat at the long table—one of Keevan's first furniture projects—several scraps of paper, a pen, and a Bible spread out in front of him. He glanced up as Keevan entered, the lamplight glinting in his gray hair. "I almost have it decoded."

Keevan slid into a chair and waited. Finally, General Stewart set down the pen, read it through one more time, and handed his decoded message across the table.

Taking it, Keevan read it quickly. Then read it again, more slowly, to make sure he'd understood it correctly. "This can't be right."

"I double-checked several times. That's what the message says." General Stewart glanced from his decoded message to the original still resting on the table in front of him.

"And Lord Alistair thinks he can trust this Blade?" Keevan still stared at the note in front of him. It didn't seem possible. A Blade had presented himself to Lord Alistair, claiming he wanted to switch sides because Keevan's cousins had helped him during the winter. All to protect them from the First Blade who now threatened them.

It had to be some kind of trap. There was no way a Blade would ever turn like that.

"He's being cautious. He isn't trusting him with any of our secrets, and he's having Lord Shadrach travel with him." General Stewart's frown stayed on his face.

It wasn't cautious enough. Lord Alistair risked his own son's life.

Keevan closed his eyes, still feeling the smooth sides of the cradle beneath his fingers. How could a father risk his child like that? Perhaps it was different when that child was grown and a man only a few years younger than Keevan.

But Keevan still couldn't fathom it. Not when all he wanted to do was dash up the stairs, wrap his arms around Addie, and bury his face in her hair until he was sure both she and their child were safe.

"Whatever was going to happen, it already has." General Stewart leaned back in his chair.

That was the hardest part about Eagle Heights. It took a fast rider a week to reach Eagle Heights from Walden. Sometimes longer if he was delayed. It would take less than that for Lord Alistair to travel to Stetterly. Whatever the Blade had been planning, he'd probably done it already. Shadrach Alistair might be dead for all they knew.

Keevan wouldn't know until Lord Alistair sent another message.

DESTROY

Keevan stepped from the main cabin as Shadrach Alistair swung from the horse. It wasn't his usual chestnut, but a dark brown.

General Stewart reached Shadrach first. "I see that Blade didn't kill you."

"No." Shadrach grinned. "Actually, I have quite the story to tell."

Keevan led the way into the meeting room. He took the head of the table while Shadrach and General Stewart sat on either side of him.

Shadrach leaned back in the chair. "That Blade my father wrote about? Turns out he was telling the truth. Respen planned to assassinate all the nobles he even suspected of supporting the Resistance."

General Stewart straightened. "Did he succeed? It would cripple us."

Keevan squeezed his fingers into fists. Had more people died for this Resistance? To keep Keevan safe here at Eagle Heights?

"No. Thanks to the Blade, we were able to warn everyone. I don't know how many took precautions and survived, but they were warned." For a moment, Shadrach's grin faltered. But he regained it as he clasped his hands behind his head. "At Walden, we killed the First Blade."

"The First Blade?" Keevan could barely rasp the words. The First Blade had killed Keevan's family. And now he was dead.

"Yes. I suspect he wasn't the only Blade killed that night. The first blow to reclaim Acktar has been struck." Shadrach sat forward and leaned his elbows on the table, a move that reminded Keevan of Lord Alistair.

Keevan clenched and unclenched his fingers. After all these years, the war seemed real and far too near. Was it possible that the Resistance could fight back? That he could reclaim his throne? Soon?

"There is one thing..." Shadrach looked away, as if he wasn't sure how Keevan would react. "My father offered the Blade refuge in Eagle Heights for helping us."

"What?" Keevan's throat closed. Why would Lord Alistair promise that of all things? Did he think they could bring a Blade here?

Addie. Their child. Keevan shook at the thought of a Blade getting anywhere near them. He could see Addie, her throat slit as his had been, curling in a puddle of her own blood.

"He's on our side now. In more ways than one. He's become a Christian."

A Blade? A Christian? Keevan couldn't put those two words together. It had to be some kind of trick. A means to get one of Respen's Blades into their confidence.

"Where is he now?" General Stewart gripped the hilt of his sword, his eyes scanning the room as if he thought the Blade might materialize out of the shadows. General Stewart had spent four and a half years protecting Keevan from Blades. He'd risked his own life to stay at Nalgar Castle to help more people flee and to prevent Respen from discovering Keevan's survival. Would he jeopardize that now and let a Blade in their sanctuary here at Eagle Heights?

"At Nalgar Castle." Shadrach blew out a long breath. "He returned to continue spying."

Either he was really brave or he was returning to report to Respen.

One could save them. The other could kill them all.

Lord Alistair might have decided to trust this Blade, but ultimately, the decision would rest with Keevan. And if he chose wrong, he'd answer to all the innocent lives sheltered here at Eagle Heights.

REFUGEES POURED INTO EAGLE HEIGHTS—MORE THAN EVER before—with stories of armies and destruction. Addie could see the doubt in Keevan's eyes every time he received a new report. Was this the time to fight back as they had planned for the past four years? Or was it already too late? Had they waited too long?

Keevan's cousins were prisoners at Nalgar Castle. Walter Esroy, their best scout and message rider, lay dead in a grave somewhere in the Hills.

Their mountain wasn't big enough to hold all the people nor would their supplies last, especially now that Walden would soon be under siege, if not overrun, and there would be no more supplies coming.

Addie gripped Keevan's arm as they navigated down the path from the top of Eagle Heights to the village at the bottom where the latest group of refugees were being given whatever temporary shelter they could muster.

She rubbed her free hand along her back. This trail had been a lot easier before she'd been pregnant. Now, she couldn't see her own feet. She could imagine her brothers, trailing behind them, laughing under their breaths. She didn't turn around to look.

"You don't have to come." Keevan halted them and steered her to a boulder. "You should be resting."

"I'm tired of resting." Addie sank onto the boulder anyway. "I'll be fine in a minute."

"I'm still going to find a horse and have you ride on the way back. Either that, or I'm going to carry you."

Addie closed her eyes, trying to imagine Keevan staggering under her weight. He'd probably tip over backwards and send them careening down the hill. "Find a horse, please. I highly doubt you can carry me at the moment."

"Really?" Keevan's eyes twinkled, and that was enough warning for Addie to brace herself before he looped one arm around her back and the other under her knees. When he tried to pick her up, he staggered and nearly dropped her.

She wrapped her arms around his neck. "Put me down before you hurt yourself."

Over Keevan's shoulder, she caught sight of her brothers. Frank had his arms stretched out, as if prepared to catch the two of them if Keevan collapsed. Brennen shrugged while Patrick bent over, laughing.

"I'm fine." Keevan gasped as he straightened, heaving her higher as he tottered a step down the trail. "You're not that heavy."

He was lying. She was only a few inches shorter than him, and, pregnant as she was, she wasn't exactly small or light.

Still, if he wanted to hurt himself, she wasn't going to argue. Not when it spared her aching feet and back. Though, being half-curled in his arms was making it hard to breathe.

He made it to the bottom of the slope before, arms shaking, he set her back on her feet. As he bent over, hands on knees, to catch his breath, Addie patted his arm. "We'll be taking a horse back."

"Yes." Between his panting and his rasp, the word was barely intelligible.

When his breathing steadied, he held out an arm to her again. "Shall we make a more proper entrance?"

She took it and pasted on the smile she'd practiced for the past two years at Keevan's side. A small enough smile that she could hold it for hours without her face hurting, yet large enough to seem welcoming.

By the time they broke through the last few trees into the cleared dirt that counted as the road through a row of cabins, she and Keevan were composed and serene. Behind them, her brothers remained stiff, outwardly the picture of a prince's royal guards. Inwardly, they were probably plotting ways to tug her hair out of her bun.

She greeted each of the new families, focusing so that she could remember as many names as possible.

Beneath her hand, Keevan stiffened. He gaped at a family a few yards away.

Frank stepped beside Keevan, hand on his sword's hilt. "What is it?"

Patrick appeared beside Addie, easing around her to put his shoulder in front of her. Behind them, Brennen closed in a few steps.

Keevan released a shuddering breath. "Frank, I need to talk to that couple up ahead privately. Is there a place nearby?"

Frank let go of his sword and nodded at the cabin across the street. "I'll see if that one is open. Patrick, can you escort them?"

Patrick strode away, leaving Addie's side feeling cold.

Frank waved them over to the cabin, and Addie let Keevan lead her inside. She blinked as her eyes adjusted to the faint lamplight after the brilliance of the summer sun outside.

Footsteps pounded outside, then the door swung open. Patrick strode inside, followed by a slim man with brown hair and beard who glared at Keevan and a young woman, who twisted her fingers together in front of her as if she couldn't decide whether she wanted to run or be sick.

What would cause such reactions in them? Most of the time when the refugees realized Keevan was alive, they were astounded.

But these people only looked angry.

"Your Highness." The young man gave a stiff nod of his head, as if that was all the bow he would deign to give Keevan.

Keevan squeezed his eyes shut, his scar standing out stark in the lamplight. When he opened his eyes again, his gaze focused on the young woman. "Ellenora, isn't it? Five and a half years ago, I hurt you."

Both the young man and woman flinched. Addie had seen the reaction before, the way people recoiled from the monstrous sound of Keevan's damaged voice.

But this time, she flinched too as the pieces nailed together. This woman standing in front of her was the one Keevan had told her about. Addie didn't want to imagine him pulling this girl into a closet, kissing her...

She slammed away the thoughts. Keevan wasn't that boy anymore.

"I hurt you, and I was wrong. I would ask for your

forgiveness, but I understand if you can't give it." Keevan gaze dipped to the floor.

Addie squeezed his arm tighter. She had to let him know he wasn't facing his past alone.

The woman, Ellenora, shuddered, her fingers still fidgeting. "You were young, and I never should've—"

The young man opened his mouth, but Keevan beat him to it. "Don't blame yourself and don't make excuses for me. I was old enough to know what I was doing, and I was your prince. That didn't give you much choice. I know it doesn't mean much now, but I am sorry, and I'm doubly sorry that, thanks to my father, I didn't receive the punishment I rightly deserved for my actions."

As hard as this was to hear and as much as Addie wished she was anywhere but in this room, she slipped her hand into Keevan's and squeezed. He'd done wrong, but he wasn't making any excuses.

Ellenora hugged her arms to her stomach, finally stilling her frantic fingers. "It took me a long time to trust again."

The young man—her husband, Addie guessed—wrapped his arm around her waist. He still glared at Keevan like he wanted to punch him.

Addie would've hugged both of them, but she didn't think they would want a hug from her.

"I still live with the memories." Ellenora glanced up, something in her face smoothing. "But, somehow, I think you understand what it's like to live with a scar."

Keevan gave a small nod, and the lamplight shone against the long white scar running across his cheek and down onto his neck. A scar he couldn't hide, not on his face, and not in his voice.

Addie couldn't be sure which scars were worse. The ones that could be hidden or the ones that couldn't.

"If you wish, I will order myself punished for what I did back then." A shiver ran down Keevan's back.

Addie traced her hand along his spine. Was there a punishment for his crime? As far as Addie knew, being caught kissing in a linen closet was scandalous and wrong, but not something against the law. If there was a punishment, it would be in that law book Keevan read over and over again, though Addie hadn't made it through the first couple of pages.

But Addie could imagine what her papa would have done to any of her brothers if they'd been caught doing what Keevan had done. They would've been cleaning the castle privies for a year, and that would be the enjoyable part of the punishment.

"Do it." The young man crossed his arms.

"No." Ellenora released a long, slow breath, placed a hand on her husband's arm, and turned to Keevan. "No, I think you have been punished enough. I forgave you years ago when I thought the Blades had killed you, and it no longer seemed right to hate a dead boy. And I forgive you now."

"Thank you."

Addie leaned her head against Keevan's shoulder. Perhaps now, Keevan would finally be able to let go of some of the guilt that still plagued him.

"Now may we go? Or are you going to detain us further?" The young man scowled, as if hoping Keevan would still give him a reason to throw that first punch.

"No, you may go. Thank you for taking the time to speak with me."

The young man steered his wife from the cabin, slamming the door behind them.

Addie turned, wrapped her arms around Keevan, and leaned against him as much as she could while nearly six months pregnant. Beyond the beating of Keevan's heart, shuffling filled the room. Her brothers leaving to give them a bit of privacy.

As one, probably Patrick, slipped past her, a hand tugged her hairpin free, sending her hair springing out of its bun.

10

"Good shot, Patrick. You're getting better."

Keevan ducked a swing from Frank and risked a glance toward the tree several of his bodyguards, including Patrick and Brennen, were using as a target. Patrick had gotten within an inch of the center of the knot where a branch had once been.

"Are you kidding? That was a great shot!" Patrick shook his head and nocked another arrow, as if to prove that shot wasn't a one-time wonder.

The flat of a sword whacked against Keevan's shin. "Pay attention."

Keevan would've dragged his attention back to Frank and their sword fight, but a man sprinted from the direction of the entrance to Eagle Heights. General Stewart spoke with him for a few minutes before turning and hurrying toward Keevan.

"I think we'll have to halt." Keevan sheathed his sword. Around him, the others dropped what they were doing and gathered around him, going from friends to guards. Seven of his personal guards were there: Addie's three brothers, and four of the men who'd helped get Keevan out of Nalgar all those years ago.

Addie set aside her sewing and let Brennen pull her to her feet and into the cluster of guards. Keevan reached a hand toward her, and she slid her fingers into his. He wasn't sure why his stomach dropped like it did.

General Stewart halted in front of him. "Shadrach Alistair is outside the entrance. He has a Blade with him. He requests sanctuary for him."

Keevan closed his eyes. Sanctuary for a Blade. What choice did he have? Lord Alistair had promised the Blade refuge for turning against Respen. Keevan couldn't break Lord Alistair's word and his own integrity by turning the Blade away, especially not when he stood outside the stones of Eagle Heights.

But what if this was an elaborate trap? What if getting a Blade into Eagle Heights had been Respen's plan all along? Keevan had thousands of lives depending on him to keep them safe here. Including his wife and unborn child.

"Let them enter, but keep a watch on the Blade. I want to speak with him and Shadrach Alistair in the meeting room." Keevan straightened his shoulders. He could face this Blade. Somehow.

Spinning on his heels, Keevan marched toward the main cabin as quickly as Addie's pace would allow. As soon as they were inside, Keevan gripped her arms. "Please go upstairs. I don't want that Blade getting anywhere near you."

Addie kissed his cheek right over the scar. "All right."

As she climbed up one step at a time, Keevan faced her

brothers. "I want the three of you stationed here at the bottom of the stairs. Don't let anyone past besides me."

Frank rested a hand on his sword while Patrick and Brennen took up positions on either side of him. Even Patrick didn't smile.

The other four guards gathered around him. Keevan drew in a deep breath. This was going to be hard enough to face without an audience. He pointed at the door across the hall. "Wait there if you're needed."

"But, sir..." Oran stared at him, wide-eyed, as General Stewart stepped inside.

"I don't think this Blade will try anything here." Keevan had to believe that. "General Stewart, I'd like you to escort Shadrach Alistair and the Blade into the meeting room and stay when I speak with them."

Keevan didn't wait for a reply. He strode into the room. A few candles burned at the far end, and Keevan began to light a few more, but his hands were shaking.

In a few minutes, he would face a Blade for the first time in four and a half years. And he would have to be civil. Surely he could do that. He would have to interview this Blade, judge if he was telling the truth, and make a decision from there.

Be objective. Be a leader. Don't let his emotions get the better of him. Wasn't that what he'd spent these past four years learning?

Voices echoed outside the door. Keevan faced the wall, staring at the flickering candle flames.

A knock sounded against the door. Keevan drew in a deep breath. It was time. "Come in."

Three sets of feet tromped across the floorboards.

Keevan couldn't make himself turn around. Perhaps if he didn't look at the Blade, he could get through this.

"Your Highness."

Maybe if Keevan pretended only Shadrach stood behind him, he would survive this. "Welcome, Lord Shadrach. What news do you bring of Acktar?"

"Respen's armies have attacked Walden. My father and a few volunteers were besieged last time we knew."

Keevan drew in a shuddering breath. Walden under siege. Lord Alistair, the man who'd protected Keevan when his entire world had fallen apart, could be dead.

"Lady Rennelda remains a prisoner in Nalgar Castle, but Lady Brandiline was rescued and brought here."

His cousins. Keevan tried to picture them, but all he remembered was a twelve-year-old tousle-headed girl crying while her eight-year-old sister huddled behind Aunt Annita. After all these years, it was hard to remember he even had a family besides Addie's.

Shadrach paused, and the pause was long enough to wrap tension through Keevan's stomach and down his back. He could sense the Blade behind him. Sense the Blade's eyes studying him.

"The Blade I told you about, the one that defected to our side months ago, has been forced to flee Acktar."

Keevan had to face him. He couldn't keep cowering with his face turned to the wall. Clenching his fists, Keevan spun on his heel.

His gaze slammed into a pair of bright green eyes set in a tanned face below black hair. The same green eyes he'd once seen peering down at him, knife glinting in the moonlight.

That knife. The tearing, searing pain. Terror. Steel shining and flashing as it stabbed down...

And Addie. Addie and their unborn child were in this cabin. Too close to this Blade. To his knives slashing...slashing...Addie's throat...her blood pumping onto white sheets...

"Arrest him." The words rasped from Keevan's throat. He had to get this Blade away from Addie. Away from their child. He was too free, standing there untied within reach of his weapons. Keevan had to make sure those knives couldn't get anywhere near Addie.

His gasps joined a roaring in his ears. Addie. Their child. And only a staircase separating them from this Blade.

"No, you don't understand." Shadrach threw himself between the Blade and Keevan, as if the Blade was the one who needed protecting. "Leith saved my father's life and the lives of all the nobility still loyal to you. He may have been a Blade but not anymore."

Leith. That was this monster's name.

Shadrach was the one who didn't understand. He didn't have memories of moonlight and knives and green eyes and pain, so much pain. Choking and terror and death squeezing the life from his throat and knowing that all his brothers had died the same way, even thirteen-year-old Duncan.

"Shad, don't." The Blade, the killer named Leith, laid a hand on Shadrach's arm. "He has reason to arrest me. I'm the Blade who gave him that scar."

His voice was a low baritone, unhindered as it came from his mouth. Would Keevan's voice have sounded like that had this Blade not stolen it when he'd tried to steal his life?

Shadrach stiffened, his gaze flicking between Keevan and the Blade. Apparently, he hadn't guessed the connection.

But someone had known. Surely Lord Alistair had guessed this Blade Leith was the one who'd nearly killed Keevan. He'd read Keevan's description of him. He'd seen the same note from Stetterly that Keevan had. The moment this Blade met his gaze, Lord Alistair had to have known.

Yet he'd kept this secret from Keevan, his prince, his Leader. Instead, he'd let this Blade walk right into Eagle Heights.

Heat burned along Keevan's spine and into his scar. He had to cross his arms to hide his shaking hands. Lord Alistair had sworn his loyalty to Keevan. Keevan had trusted Lord Alistair to lead the Resistance in Acktar on his behalf. Yet, Lord Alistair had chosen this monster.

Except the monster seemed intent on not acting like one. He stepped forward, knelt, and clasped his hand over his heart. "My king."

Such a lie. Where had his loyalty been when he'd brought the knife down? When he'd helped kill Uncle Laurence and Aunt Annita? Keevan didn't have to take such tainted words, not from the likes of him.

He clenched his fingers. "How many marks do you have, Blade?"

The Blade pushed his sleeve to his shoulder, showing off rows upon rows of marks from his shoulder to his elbow. Such small marks for all the blood they carried.

"Thirty-seven." The Blade's shoulders rose and fell as he pointed at a mark on his upper arm. "Killing you was my sixth mark, though it seems I was less successful than either Respen or I realized."

Which mark was Uncle Laurence's and Aunt Annita's?

How many other deaths were recorded there? Twenty? More?

And Shadrach expected Keevan to simply turn this Blade loose in Eagle Heights? A mountain filled with women and children who had already seen too much pain?

Keevan gestured to General Stewart, who had slowly stalked behind the Blade. "General, take him away."

The Blade, slippery snake that he was, meekly held up his hands. He didn't struggle as General Stewart yanked his hands behind his back more roughly than necessary. General Stewart had the same memories of blood and knives on a moonlit night. He, at least, understood.

"What do you plan to do with him?" Shadrach gripped those knives as if he contemplated interfering and making his family's betrayal even more complete.

"Hold a trial. I'm sure I'll be able to find a few eyewitnesses to provide testimony." Keevan hadn't given it much thought, yet. But surely the thousands of families here at Eagle Heights deserved justice. Surely he deserved justice.

Shadrach glared. "You can't do that. He could be sentenced to death. He came here seeking mercy. My father promised him sanctuary in good faith."

Lord Alistair had also kept the truth from Keevan. Where had his promises of loyalty been then? "Your father had no right to promise for me."

"He had every right." Shadrach faced Keevan like he was prepared to fight his prince over the monster. "You gave him the authority to lead the Resistance in Acktar in your place. That gives him the authority to make promises in your stead."

Keevan didn't care. Not when he could still see his own

blood dripping onto a white sheet. Not when his wife and unborn child huddled upstairs.

"A trial won't be necessary. I'm guilty. I'll confess everything, all thirty-seven marks. I have nothing I wish to hide." The Blade's voice remained even. No excuses. Just a confession of guilt.

He lifted his gaze to Keevan's. There was something in that gaze, something Keevan recognized all too well. It was the same plea for mercy that Keevan had worn only two weeks ago when facing Ellenora.

Keevan should give mercy the way he'd been granted mercy such a short time ago. He should be able to look this Blade in the eye and tell him he was forgiven.

But any thought of forgiveness drowned in the memories of the last time he'd faced this Blade. Back then, their roles had been reversed. Keevan had been the one pleading for mercy.

And this Blade hadn't given it.

He'd brought the knife down.

All the Blades had brought their knives down. And blood had filled Nalgar Castle until its cobblestones cried red.

Rorin. Aengus. Their parents. Uncle Laurence and Aunt Annita. Both of Shadrach Alistair's grandfathers. And Duncan. *Thirteen*-year-old Duncan.

Where had mercy been then?

There had been none. And there would be none now.

Keevan flicked his hand, and General Stewart dragged the Blade from the room.

Shadrach stepped in front of Keevan. "That isn't necessary!"

"Yes, it is!" Keevan clenched his fists. If he wasn't the

prince, he would've been tempted to punch Shadrach. Instead, he had to stand here and take it. "Why are you defending him?"

"Because he's my friend!" Shadrach's hands shook around the bundle of the Blade's knives, as if he didn't realize that one of those knives he held had nearly killed his prince.

"He took my voice. He helped kill my aunt and uncle." Keevan stepped closer to Shadrach. "How do you know he didn't kill one of your grandfathers?"

Shadrach exhaled a long, slow breath. His shoulders slumped a fraction. "I don't. I've never asked."

"Why not? Afraid of the answer?" Keevan crossed his arms.

"No. At this moment, it wouldn't make a difference." Shadrach switched the bundle of weapons to his other hand. "I trust him."

But Keevan didn't. How could he when all he could see was that glinting, stabbing knife over and over again? Shadrach wouldn't be so quick to trust if he'd seen the cruelty in that knife.

How could Shadrach and his father side with this Blade against Keevan?

Heat pressed into Keevan's skull and flared down his scar. And once again, that knife glinted. The green eyes hardened. And the pain choked out his life.

Keevan had to live for the rest of his life with a scar on his face and a monster in his voice. He had to wonder if each day was the one his voice would fail completely or if, when his child was born, he or she would recoil from him the same way everyone else but Addie did when they first heard him speak. Why was Keevan the one who had to endure the punishment of that night while that Blade never suffered anything for it?

When a girl with streaming red-blond hair and raised fists flew into the room, Keevan didn't control his emotions. For the second time in his life, he didn't even try.

And for the second time, he regretted it.

11

Addie leaned closer to the mirror. Her curls weren't cooperating. The summer heat sent them frizzing into a ball around her head. Nothing would tame them at this point.

Why did her hair always have to misbehave on the days she most wanted to make an impression? This was her first time meeting any of Keevan's family. Lady Brandiline was the daughter of a lord. Would she think Addie too undignified to be a princess? Would she be able to tell Addie had been born a scullery maid just by looking at her?

Keevan's footsteps paused in the doorway. "You look beautiful."

"No, I don't. I'm six months pregnant, and my hair is doing its best to touch the ceiling." Addie held out a length of leather cord. "I think it's going to take two of us to tie it back."

Keevan took the cord and strode behind her. While Addie held her hair with both hands, he wrapped the cord around her hair and knotted it tightly. "There. Is it too tight?"

"No, it's perfect." Addie let go of her hair, and grimaced at herself in the mirror. The knot might be perfect, but she wasn't. Her face shone wet and sweaty with the heat, her hair frizzed above and below the cord, and she couldn't walk without a slight waddle to her step. "Do you think she'll like me?"

Keevan wrapped his arms around her and pulled her against him. "She'll love you. She's mad at me, but she'll like you, I'm sure."

He buried his face in her hair, as if he found her sweaty, frizzy hair attractive. Go figure.

There was no accounting for taste, and she wasn't much better. After all, she found his scratchy, raspy voice attractive when almost everyone else cringed when he talked.

Stepping back, Keevan held out his arm and steadied her as they lumbered from the room and eased down the stairs. Instead of going into the meeting room, they entered the opposite door to the kitchen and dining room.

Lady Brandiline already slouched in a chair by the table, her red-blond hair in a braid down her back and her arms crossed. A boy sat in the chair beside her, shoulders and head hunched so much Addie couldn't see his eyes through his mop of wavy brown hair.

As they closed the door behind them, Lady Brandiline jabbed a finger at the boy next to her and glared at Keevan. "This is Jamie. He's a...a Blade trainee. I invited him, so you can't toss him out or lock him up or anything."

Beside Addie, Keevan stiffened.

Addie forced herself to smile. It would be up to her to

ease the tension. Somehow. She tugged Keevan a step closer to the table. How should she introduce herself? As Princess Adelaide? Even after a year and a half, the title still seemed too new, too formal. "I'm Addie. I married your cousin. Welcome to Eagle Heights, Brandiline, and I'm glad you and your friend could be here."

Brandiline huffed and scowled. "It's Brandi."

Keevan held out a chair, and Addie eased onto it. Keevan hadn't been exaggerating when he'd said his cousin was mad at him. Furious would've been a better word.

But something about Brandi relaxed the tension in Addie's chest. This wasn't the pretentious daughter of a nobleman who would expect Addie to act with the decorum befitting a princess. The girl before her had already tossed decorum out the window.

"Of course. Brandi. That's so much better than Brandiline, isn't it? My name is Adelaide, but I'd rather go by Addie. It fits me better." Addie's smile wasn't forced this time. She had two little sisters of her own. She could handle Brandi.

Brandi swung her gaze to Addie, something about her posture softening. "When people call me Brandiline, they look at me like they expect me to wear frilly pink dresses with lots of lace and act lady-like and stuff like that. Not that pink is a bad color on its own, but not when it's all fancied up."

Addie grinned. She and Brandi would get along just fine.

IT WAS LIKE SEEING AUNT ANNITA AS A CHILD. KEEVAN CUT into his portion of venison roast, letting Addie keep up most of the conversation with Brandi.

Brandi had Uncle Laurence's hair and the fire of his anger, but her eyes...the twinkle in them was all Aunt Annita. Even the way she moved, with a bounce and a flourish, was like seeing Aunt Annita again.

Someday he'd tell her how much she reminded him of her mother, but Keevan didn't think Brandi would appreciate him talking to her. Not with the way her hand tightened on her knife every time she glanced in his direction.

At least she seemed to like Addie well enough, as Keevan had known she would.

The boy—the Blade trainee—silently tucked away his food as if he knew he shouldn't be there and wanted more than anything to bolt. Keevan would've been tempted to help him along, but there had been something in the one glimpse of the boy's blue eyes he'd gotten that reminded him of Duncan. And, for that, the boy could stay.

A knock thunked against the door a moment before Patrick stepped inside. He strode to Keevan's side and leaned over to whisper, "I'm sorry to interrupt, but Shadrach Alistair is here to see you."

Apparently Patrick's whisper wasn't quiet enough. Brandi smirked and shoveled in a bite of venison as if to pretend she hadn't been eavesdropping.

"Again?" Keevan scowled. He thought he'd made his position clear an hour ago when he'd last talked to Shadrach Alistair. And the time before that. And before that.

"He never left from last time." Patrick's expression was half a grin, half a scowl.

Annoying, mule-headed, loyal lord's son.

Keevan could have Patrick tell Shadrach he was in the middle of dining with his family. But, Shadrach would probably keep camping out on the front step of the main cabin. "Have him step inside, and I'll talk to him."

As Patrick left, Keevan stood. "I'll only be a minute or two."

Addie glanced his way, nodded, and went back to asking Brandi about horses.

Keevan slipped into the entry hall as Patrick came in with Shadrach. Keevan didn't wait for him to get started on yet another endless speech about how heroic and brave and good that Blade Leith Torren was. "You are bordering on insubordination."

"I know." Shadrach crossed his arms and planted his feet in the center of the hall, as if determined he wasn't going to budge unless Keevan called an army to force him to move. "Leith Torren isn't—"

"Enough!" Keevan held up his hand. He'd heard more than enough about Leith Torren. Several times, in fact.

The worst part of it was that Shadrach was partially right. Keevan couldn't hold a trial and execute Leith Torren, much as he wanted to. Lord Alistair had given his word, and that word held as much weight as if Keevan had given the promise himself.

But Shadrach was partially wrong as well. Keevan couldn't simply turn Torren loose to wander Eagle Heights freely. All he had was Shadrach's word that Torren wasn't a danger.

And with several thousand lives—including Addie's—

resting on this decision, Keevan couldn't afford the possibility that Shadrach could be wrong.

But Shadrach simply refused to see it that way.

Keevan crossed his arms and matched Shadrach's stance. He had been lenient with Shadrach so far, but he had to be the Leader sometimes. And insisting that Shadrach comply with this decision, no matter how much he didn't like it, was one of those times. "Lord Shadrach, I have listened to your appeals several times. I have taken them into consideration, but I still believe keeping the Blade Leith Torren properly confined is the best solution."

"But, sire..."

Keevan held up a hand again. He wasn't in the mood to listen to yet another list of Leith Torren's heroic exploits. Shadrach might not listen to any explanation of caution, but Keevan had one argument left. "I know you don't like it, but this decision is as much for Leith Torren's safety as everyone else's."

That snapped Shadrach's mouth shut.

"There are several thousand people here at Eagle Heights who don't like Blades any more than I do. What do you think would happen if I turned Leith Torren loose? I would rather not find out, nor do I want to spend my time subduing a riot when we have more important things to worry about." Keevan held Shadrach's gaze, ignoring the crick he was getting in his neck due to the several inches of height Shadrach had on him. Surely Shadrach wasn't so stubborn that he'd refuse to see the logic in that.

Shadrach's shoulders slumped. "I see."

Finally.

"But..."

Keevan had to clench his fists not to punch something. Or someone.

"It's Sunday tomorrow. May he attend the services? If he isn't dressed as a Blade, and I give you my word I won't leave his side." Shadrach's expression remained blank, except for the tiniest curve to the corner of his mouth.

Shadrach had him. Keevan couldn't refuse. Not without looking like he was keeping either a fellow Christian or a killer in need of saving from hearing the word of God. "Very well, but his hands must remain securely tied. Remember, it's a precaution for his safety."

Not that Keevan cared about Leith Torren's safety. But it was the only argument that worked with Shadrach, and Keevan didn't want to find out what he'd choose if asked to stop a mob from harming Torren. A good leader should put doing what was right above his own personal feelings.

Keevan wasn't sure he was there yet.

"Thank you, Your Highness." Shadrach bowed and spun on his heels. As he left, he had to pause a moment to let General Stewart enter.

After the door closed, General Stewart turned to Keevan. "Asking about the Blade again?"

"Yes." Keevan grimaced. "Shadrach Alistair is annoyingly loyal to his friends."

General Stewart shook his head. "Annoying as it is, you can't complain too much about the Alistair loyalty. You're alive because of it."

"It's a little harder to take when used for a killer like Torren." Keevan sighed and let himself slump against the wall behind him. "I think I just allowed him to take a Blade to church."

"It could be an opportunity to observe the Blade. See if he appears genuine."

Keevan hadn't considered that. Though, if this Blade was keeping up an act, he had been good enough to fool both Lord Alistair and Shadrach. He probably wouldn't slip up during one church service.

Shifting his stance, Keevan tried to shake away thoughts of the Blade. "How are the preparations going?"

"We've done as much as we can without officially making a decision to assemble the army and move out. A few more days would give the blacksmiths time to make a few more swords, the leatherworkers a few more helmets and vests, but at this point, one or two swords either way isn't going to make a difference." General Stewart met Keevan's gaze. "We're ready whenever you give the order."

Keevan clenched his fists. He was stalling. He knew it. General Stewart knew it.

Could he be blamed for it? These past four years at Eagle Heights had been some of the best of his life. He didn't want them to end, and he wasn't ready to plunge into the war. It would be so much easier to ignore what was happening in Acktar and just live like this. Quiet dinners in this cabin. Time spent with Addie by the mountain lakes.

Nalgar Castle no longer seemed like home. Even Acktar was far away beyond a vast wilderness of valleys and mountains and cliffs.

Was one more day of peace and happiness too much to ask?

12

Addie's off-key alto warbled next to Keevan, though Keevan would never tell her how horribly she sang, not for all the cattle in Acktar. What she lacked in singing ability, she made up in enthusiasm, and that's what counted.

Especially since she sang for both of them.

Keevan held the songbook during the worship service on the mountaintop, mouthing the words to the song even if he couldn't sing them. His voice couldn't hold the resonance necessary to string words into song.

That was a secret only Addie and her family knew. The Blade had stolen his ability to sing when he'd nearly taken Keevan's voice and life. Most of the time, Keevan was too grateful he could still talk that not being able to sing didn't bother him.

But at that moment, that Blade shared a songbook with Keevan's cousin at the back of the crowd, singing.

Singing as if it didn't matter that he still *could* sing while Keevan couldn't.

As if he was the one that belonged, and Keevan was the one pretending.

Why couldn't Leith Torren stop this pretense and show everyone what he really was? A cold-hearted monster who had sneaked into Keevan's bedchamber and slashed his throat.

Keevan couldn't ignore Leith Torren's presence, try as he might to concentrate on the service. There was a Blade only a few rows behind him, only a few dozen yards away from Addie. How could Keevan concentrate on anything but that?

By the time the service ended, all Keevan wanted to do was order the guards to hustle Leith Torren back to the prison cave and away from Addie as quickly as possible.

But before he could, hoofbeats rattled against the gravel as a rider urged his horse up the slope to the mountaintop. As he swung down from the horse, the crowd parted to let him hurry toward Keevan.

Addie's grip on Keevan's arm tightened. At this point, any news that urgent couldn't be good. Had Walden fallen? Had Respen sent his Blades into the Hills? What if Respen's army was even now on their way toward Eagle Heights?

The rider halted in front of Keevan and saluted. "Sir."

"Your report?" Out of the corner of his eye, Keevan spotted General Stewart a few feet away, also listening.

"Our man in Flayin Falls got word that Respen Felix plans to marry Lady Rennelda Faythe in two weeks. He has called the nobles to come to Nalgar Castle to recognize him as the rightful Eirdon king after the marriage."

Keevan's breath caught in his throat.

He'd waited too long. He'd thought he had time, a little of it anyways. But he'd been fooling himself. There was no time. Perhaps there never had been.

Would this shake the Resistance? Would some of his allies switch sides because of this? As far as they knew, the Eirdon heir they had been rallying behind all these years was Keevan's cousin Renna. Surely they would come back to his side once they realized Keevan was the Leader.

But would it be too late?

It was already too late for Renna.

Keevan had gone over this with General Stewart when they'd discussed various attack plans the past several months. Keevan's army would take two weeks to even reach the edge of the Sheered Rock Hills, and even that was a faster march than General Stewart would've liked to put the men through before battle.

He swept his gaze over the cabins, the ring of boulders and spires surrounding the mountaintop, the clear, unimpeded sky. No matter how much Keevan wanted to stay, he had to gather his war council and plan his return to Acktar.

His gaze snagged on a slim figure at the back of the crowd staring his way. Leith Torren.

Keevan suppressed a growl. Much as he wanted to, he got the feeling he wouldn't be able to keep the Blade out of the discussion.

KEEVAN RESTED HIS HEAD IN HIS HANDS. THE MEETING ROOM had gone silent now that his war council had left to carry out their tasks. Only General Stewart remained, sitting to

Keevan's right. Even though General Stewart would probably be up half the night to ready the army, he still stayed.

Addie and her family were Keevan's home, but General Stewart was Keevan's rock. He'd stood with Keevan since the beginning.

"Do you trust him?" Keevan rasped the words through his aching throat. After the hours of discussion, his voice was deserting him. He would need Addie's ministrations to make sure he could talk tomorrow morning.

"Yes." General Stewart didn't even hesitate.

That's what Keevan thought. After Leith Torren volunteered to return to Nalgar and a week of torture to buy Keevan time to rescue Renna, who wouldn't believe him? No matter how much he had been pressured, his sincerity had been unshakable.

If only it was some kind of trick. Maybe Torren planned to betray them to Respen.

But Keevan's gut said Torren was telling the truth. No man could take what Keevan had thrown at Torren so humbly without being sincere.

"Think he'll really do it?" Keevan massaged his fingers into his throat, trying to relieve some of the pain.

"If that was Princess Adelaide at Nalgar, how far would you go to get her back?" General Stewart leaned back in his chair, arms crossed.

Yes, Keevan would face a week of torture for Addie. But would he volunteer for it with the same steel as Torren? Probably not. Keevan was too familiar with his own weaknesses. He would break under sustained torture.

But Leith Torren was a better man than Keevan.

And that made it worse.

Keevan scowled. General Stewart had compared Torren and Renna to Keevan and Addie. Had Torren gone and fallen in *love* with Keevan's cousin? What if she thought herself in love back?

If Torren survived, Keevan would never be rid of him.

Sighing, Keevan tried to sort through the churn in his stomach. He wasn't angry. Not anymore.

He was jealous.

Lord Alistair, Shadrach, Brandi, everyone tripped over themselves to forgive Torren. They seemed to think, now that Torren was redeemed, that he wouldn't fall back into killing.

But if Keevan had confessed his darkest secret? Where would be his forgiveness? There would be none. Only suspicion that Keevan might do it again.

Were he and Torren all that different? Torren had stolen lives while Keevan had stolen innocence. Yet, Torren got to move on while Keevan couldn't.

Perhaps Keevan should give Torren the forgiveness he wanted for himself. That was what a good Christian would do, wasn't it? Forgive.

But a good king fought for justice. What sort of justice could Keevan give the families of those Torren killed if he forgave him?

Was there a way to honor the promise that had been made through Lord Alistair, give forgiveness, and also uphold justice?

Maybe not. Maybe Keevan could only choose between them, but never justice and mercy at the same time.

General Stewart cleared his throat, reminding Keevan

that he still sat there, arms crossed, waiting for Keevan to pull himself together and start acting like the Leader.

But how could Keevan make decisions for the whole country when he couldn't even decide on this?

Perhaps he had become his father after all. A weak king paralyzed at the thought of making the smallest choice.

He traced a hand down the length of his scar. "I honestly don't know what to do about Leith Torren."

General Stewart's gaze remained steady. "May I speak freely?"

A hint of a smile tugged at Keevan's mouth. "Surely by now, you know you're one of the few people who doesn't have to ask permission to be brutally honest with me. It's why I value your counsel."

"And sometimes, it doesn't hurt to remind you that you have a choice whether you want to hear it." General Stewart's mouth took on a similar upward twitch before he sobered. "If we succeed in reclaiming Acktar, Leith Torren's case won't be the only one you'll have to deal with. Half the nobles in Acktar betrayed you. Half the people are fighting against you. Will you hold on to bitterness for all of them? There's going to be enough bitterness already. Will you execute all your enemies? Respen has provided an example of what that looks like."

Keevan scrubbed harder at the tightness around his throat. How did he want to handle victory? Defeat would be easy. Most likely, he wouldn't be alive to see it. Or, if he was particularly cowardly, he could crawl back here.

But in victory, he would have to become king.

"The people will look to you to lead by example. What kind of example do you intend to set for them?"

"I don't know." Keevan hung his head. A better king would know what to do. He'd have a plan for reconciling the country. But Keevan was still just the lost prince struggling for a voice.

General Stewart's chair scraped as he stood. His hand rested briefly on Keevan's shoulder. "Maybe you don't know now, but you will."

Keevan couldn't lift his head to acknowledge the words. He was going to fail. He was too weak and flawed and the burden of the country was too great.

And his parents, siblings, Uncle Laurence, Aunt Annita, and everyone killed by Respen would have died in vain.

13

Addie smoothed her fingers over the green and white uniform her husband wore. So crisp and clean, it was hard to remember it signified war.

Keevan wrapped his arms around her waist and leaned his forehead against hers. "I'm going to miss this."

She didn't have to ask what he meant. This. All of it. Eagle Heights. Their cabin. The freedom to be simply Keevan and Addie occasionally.

When Keevan walked out the cabin door, he wouldn't be coming back. Either he succeeded and reclaimed his throne or he died.

Her throat closed. She might never see him again. He might die on some battlefield on Acktar's prairie, and Respen's victorious army wouldn't give him the courtesy of a decent burial.

How could she complain when so many other wives, sisters, and mothers were saying a similar goodbye in the other cabins at Eagle Heights, including her own mother, sisters, and sister-in-law? Some had sons as young as fourteen leaving. Others watched their grandfathers grab their weapons. Addie had to be an example to them just as much as Keevan was an example to his men.

This was her test as a princess. For the first time, she'd have to lead without Keevan there.

Could she do it? Or would she go back to hiding like the scullery maid she'd been?

Keevan's hands moved to rest on either side of their unborn child. "I'm not going to be there. If we win, I'll have to stay at Nalgar, and you'll be unable to travel, probably for several months after the baby is born. The journey would be too much for both of you."

Even if he won, even if he survived, their separation would be for months. Possibly half a year or more by the time the baby was old enough to make the journey through the wilds of the Sheered Rock Hills. Keevan wouldn't be there to hold his newborn. He wouldn't be there for all the firsts. The baby might not even recognize him by the time Addie could travel.

It hurt so deeply Addie couldn't even cry. After all their hopes and dreams for the beginning of their family, Keevan's duty to the kingdom forced him to miss it.

And, if he died, he'd never even see his child.

War wasn't fair. No matter the cause, it was heartless.

But sometimes, it couldn't be avoided. Duty pulled all of them to it. Everything in the past four and a half years had been in preparation for this moment. Keevan couldn't shirk from it, and Addie couldn't either. She'd agreed to this when she'd married him, knowing the country would often have to come first.

"Just stay alive. Win. We'll join you as soon as we're able." Addie tipped her face up and captured his mouth with hers. She would give anything to keep him here with her only a little longer. Another day. Another hour.

But Keevan pulled back. His duty called, and she couldn't do anything but let him go.

As he strode from the cabin and she watched him mount his palomino, gather her brothers around him, and lead his army from Eagle Heights, Addie prayed it wasn't the last time she would ever see them.

KEEVAN PRAYED AS HE TURNED HIS HORSE AROUND, HIS HANDS shaking on the reins. The battlefield lay in front of him. Dead soldiers piled in lumps marring the prairie. His blood pounded in his ears, as if to reassure him it was still in his body and not pouring from a gaping wound like so many of the soldiers staggering from the field.

Respen's army remained solid and impenetrable behind their entrenchments. The besieged town of Walden anchored their eastern flank while a fortified ridge held the western flank. Keevan's charge at the middle had done little good.

"Where's Captain Alistair?" Keevan glanced at the bluff overlooking the enemy's western flank. No movement. Not even a stir of breeze or a puff of dust.

As predicted, the enemy scouts had detected the three hundred and fifty riders circling down the Spires Canyon, led by General Stewart's son. The eastern flank had been strengthened, and by the time Captain Stewart led the charge from behind Walden, the line had wavered, but not buckled.

The western flank was weak due to all the reinforcements that had been shifted to the center and east to ward off Keevan's and Captain Stewart's charges. Now was the time to strike, if only Shadrach got in position in time.

He had to. Keevan could accept nothing else.

"Form up for another charge." Keevan steadied his horse and adjusted his grip on his sword.

General Stewart shouted the order, and it was picked up by the captains and lieutenants. While their men assembled, General Stewart eased his horse closer to Keevan and lowered his voice. "If Captain Alistair doesn't arrive in time, this charge will break like the last one, and this time, I don't think we'll recover. We'll have to retreat and regroup."

"I know." Keevan didn't turn to look at General Stewart. He couldn't afford to show even a hint of doubt. He was the Leader, and at this moment, he might be leading his men to disaster.

But at least he'd made a decision.

He straightened his shoulders. "He's an Alistair. He will do nothing less than arrive at precisely the right time."

General Stewart's saddle creaked. "The men are in position."

Keevan drew in a deep breath and let it out slowly. Once he gave the order, he was committed.

All those years ago, God had preserved his life when he should've died. Maybe he'd been kept alive for this moment to restore truth and justice to Acktar.

Or maybe that wasn't God's plan at all. Perhaps Keevan

would die here, and restoring justice would be left to his son or daughter.

Nothing Keevan could do but trust God and move forward.

He'd done so little trusting in his life. He'd either wandered without a purpose or moaned about the purpose he'd been given. He'd focused solely on himself, kicking against anything that wasn't what he wanted.

But it didn't matter what Keevan wanted. God had placed him in this position at this moment. Keevan was the Eirdon heir, even though he'd been born a second son. He'd lived, even though a Blade had been sent to kill him. He'd been given Addie's love, even though his past should've made that impossible.

Maybe victory would be possible. Keevan couldn't be sure, but duty demanded he ride forward and face whatever God had in store for him.

He glanced to either side. General Stewart was there. And the six soldiers who'd guarded him from the beginning. Addie's brothers were also there, even Samuel. Frank gave him a nod. They would ride with him no matter what.

"Charge." Keevan nudged his horse into motion without waiting for General Stewart to pass the order along.

Shouted orders rang out behind him. Then the thunder of hundreds of galloping hooves drowned out the sound of thousands of drumming feet.

Arrows arced over his head, soundless as they descended onto the enemy's line in front of him. More arrows answered, whipping past Keevan's face and his horse's flying mane.

Keevan didn't stop. He didn't flinch.

A distant sound caught his ear. He wasn't even sure how he'd heard it over the pounding of his own horse's hooves.

But there, on the far bluff, a line of men and horses poured down the slope, a shining chestnut in the lead.

Shadrach Alistair had done it.

As if sensing his renewed energy, his horse gave an extra burst of speed as they reached the trenches. Keevan knocked aside a thrusting sword and leaned sideways to avoid another. His horse lurched onto the earth embankment.

His men charged onto the earthen mound around him. General Stewart urged the soldiers onward.

Keevan kicked his own horse. He had to go forward and trust his men would follow him.

Everything was chaos. Striking, stabbing, dodging. Nothing Keevan had done in practice could've prepared him for this, not even sparring with all three of Addie's brothers at once.

But something was changing. The enemy was going backwards. Men broke from the fighting and ran. At first only a few, but then the whole line was wavering and falling back and running and...

Keevan found himself at the top of the ridge, only his men around him in the closing darkness.

Frank was next to him, unharmed except for a cut above his eye. Patrick swung down from his horse and stepped over to Keevan. "You all right?"

"Yes." Keevan eased down from his horse. His right shoulder ached, as did his arm. As he straightened, he found all the other muscles he'd pulled and overworked. He glanced around between Frank to Patrick to Brennen, who pressed a hand to a gash on his shoulder. "Where's Samuel?"

Frank stiffened and spun on his heel.

Keevan fought to push down the weight in his stomach. Of all of them, why did it have to be Samuel? "Frank, go look for him. Patrick and Brennen, you're with me."

Frank dashed into the twilight.

Keevan gripped his horse's reins. He couldn't think about Samuel now. This entire army depended on him.

General Stewart appeared out of the gloom. "Your orders, sire?"

His orders. General Stewart was looking at him as if Keevan really was the Leader. As if he expected Keevan to be the wise one.

Keevan forced his back to straighten. This was his purpose. Lead.

After four years of helping to organize refugees at Eagle Heights, he even knew what to do. "Have the captains and lieutenants organize their men into their divisions and take a roll call of those still standing to help us identify the injured and dead. Instruct the healers to set up their tents near Walden. They'll have better access to fresh water there. And we'll need stretcher bearers to carry the wounded and a burial detail to see to the dead."

"I'll see to it." General Stewart nodded and clapped Keevan on the shoulder. "You should get some rest."

Keevan shook his head. He wouldn't be able to sleep, not after the battle. Not while the screams and sobs of the wounded filled his ears. "I will later. I need to get Lord Alistair's report."

If he'd been a better leader, he would've been prepared for after the battle. He would've had healers better organized so that the response would be quicker.

"Very well." General Stewart turned to attend to his duties, but Keevan held up a hand.

"Wait, one more thing." Keevan should've thought of this earlier. "Ask the captains and lieutenants to call for volunteers with any healing experience. Even if it's only stitching wounds. Have them report to the healers by Walden. Oran, that means you too."

General Stewart nodded and strode away to carry out Keevan's instructions. Oran, the soldier who'd stitched up Keevan's wound years ago, saluted and dashed toward Walden.

Picking his way through the dead and wounded men, Keevan found Lord Alistair partway down the hill toward Walden, leaning on Shadrach's shoulder. Lord Alistair's face showed pale and gaunt beneath his straggling beard, his eyes sunken into hollows. A bandage wrapped around his right leg below the knee while his left hand hung limp from the end of a sling. Gray streaked through his hair, something that hadn't been there when Keevan had last seen him over four years ago.

For some reason, Keevan hadn't expected Lord Alistair to change, even though he'd watched Shadrach grow from a skinny teenager to a confident twenty-year-old captain. When reading Lord Alistair's reports, Keevan had seen him with his unlined face and brown hair free of gray. The furrows and gray were almost as much of a shock as the tottering steps and thin body.

Seeing him like this, it no longer mattered that Lord Alistair had hidden the truth of Leith Torren's identity. He had given his last full measure to hold Walden and keep Respen's army here. That was proof enough of his loyalty.

Lord Alistair bowed as much as he could without letting go of Shadrach's shoulder. "Your Highness."

There was something about the tone of Lord Alistair's words. He'd bowed and said something similar all those years ago, but that had been out of duty to Keevan's family name. This time, the words carried a depth, as if Lord Alistair believed Keevan deserved the title.

As if he was the Leader in more than name only.

Keevan waved at Lord Alistair's arm. "What happened?"

Lord Alistair gave a small shrug. The fingers of his hand flopped. "Part of a wall collapsed and crushed my elbow. I haven't been able to feel or move my hand since. The healer is doubtful I'll ever regain the use of it."

Keevan nodded and resisted the urge to run his fingers over his scar. He understood what it was like to lose the use of part of his body and fear he'd never regain it. "I'm sorry for your hand, but I'm grateful you survived."

Shadrach's arm tightened around Lord Alistair's back.

"If you're able, would you be willing to aid the healers in procuring water and other supplies that Walden has available?" Keevan pointed down the hill where a row of tall, white tents had already been constructed.

"Of course." Lord Alistair pulled himself straighter using Shadrach as a crutch. With another bow, he turned with Shadrach's help and tottered down the hill toward Walden.

Brennen stepped to Keevan's side, a cloth now wrapped tightly around his upper arm. "Would you like us to set up your tent?"

Keevan's men had died today. Were still dying out there on the battlefield while they waited for someone to tend their injuries. He couldn't just roll himself into his blanket and ignore them.

Maybe he should rest or perhaps gather his war council to plan the next move on their march toward Nalgar Castle. Even now, Respen's army had to be regrouping on some distant hill.

But sleep and planning didn't matter while the constant moaning and crying filled the night until even the crickets couldn't be heard.

"No. Come." Keevan set off down the hill. Even this soon after the battle, men lay in rows next to the healers' tents.

He forced himself forward and knelt next to the first man in the row. The man's hands clutched at a gaping wound across his stomach. The man's eyes widened further. "S-sir."

"Rest easy." Keevan pressed his hands over the wound.

Patrick knelt, cut off the bottom of his shirt, and wadded it over the man's wound. The look on Patrick's face confirmed what Keevan suspected. The man wouldn't last long, even with a healer's help.

Keevan met the man's eyes. "Press this to your wound, all right?"

The man managed a nod.

"Hang on. The healers will get to you soon, I'm sure." Keevan squeezed the man's shoulder before he moved on to the next man in the line. Then the next.

Keevan's eyes ached, his back and leg muscles burned with the constant bending and kneeling. But he couldn't allow himself to stop. Not until he'd spoken to every man who'd shed blood for him that day.

Maybe it was foolish to even try. There were too many, and more being brought in every minute.

But they had been willing to sacrifice everything for him. The least he could do was sacrifice a little time and rest for them.

The next soldier in line couldn't be more than sixteen. He rocked back and forth, both hands pressed to the deep gash across his face from the bottom of his ear to his mouth. Tears streamed from the boy's eyes.

Keevan rested a hand on the boy's shoulder. "You'll get a nice scar out of that."

The boy glanced up, and his eyes focused on Keevan's face, probably on the scar. He shuddered.

"I know it hurts." Keevan rested a hand on the boy's shoulder. "But the healers will be with you soon. Hold on until then, all right?"

The boy sniffed and nodded.

Keevan had to move on. He had more wounded men and boys to visit.

A few more lines of men later, he found Frank sitting beside Samuel. All the color had drained from Samuel's face, and large red spot spread along the white shirt wrapped around his middle.

Keevan sank to the ground next to them. "How bad is he?"

Samuel shifted his head. "It hurts."

"It's a bad wound, but should be all right once he receives attention." The muscle at the corner of Frank's jaw flexed.

"Do you need me to speed things along?" Keevan placed his hands on the ground to push himself to his feet. If he asked, the healers would tend Samuel next.

"No, don't." Samuel raised his hand, limply swatting at Keevan's chest. "I-I can wait. Just like everyone else."

Keevan couldn't find any words for that. He'd seen a lot of courage that day, but this was something more coming from his youngest brother-in-law. "Brennen, stay with them."

Brennen nodded and eased to the ground beside Frank.

Frank met Keevan's gaze. He understood. There had to be two of them. One to stay with Samuel and one to get help or fetch Patrick and Keevan if the worst happened.

By the time dawn broke pink and raw across the eastern horizon, Keevan swayed on his feet. But when the captains gathered their divisions for their orders, Keevan saw something else in them. Something similar to the look that had been in Lord Alistair's eyes.

Yesterday, these men had followed him into battle out of duty. Today, they followed him because they believed him worth following.

He wasn't king yet, and he hadn't won this war.

But for one night, he'd done his best.

And it had been enough.

14

Four long days of fighting. Three long nights of visiting the wounded. Keevan could count the hours of sleep he'd gotten on one hand.

If he had the energy to concentrate that much.

And now he crept along the bottom of the dry moat with his soldiers at his back, peering at the dark silhouette of the Tower looming against the faded, twilight sky and preparing to face the traitor Respen Felix.

Shouldn't he have felt more prepared for this? Ready? Excited to be finally facing Respen and taking back the country?

He was just...tired. The kind of tired where his bones ached and his eyelids scratched. His muscles shook with the strain of keeping himself standing.

But if they didn't move tonight, his cousin Renna would die. They'd lose the distraction Leith Torren had volunteered to buy them with his torture.

After all these years, what would it be like to face

Respen? Respen had been the faceless monster lurking in the shadows for so long. He'd killed Keevan's entire family, but Keevan couldn't remember ever meeting him. Could he handle looking into the man's eyes without losing his steel?

Please grant me strength. Keevan breathed out the prayer, and his muscles eased. Whatever happened in the coming battle, win or lose, God was with Keevan, and God's will would be done.

Keevan followed the curve of the moat until the wooden bridge connecting the Tower to the rest of the castle rose above his head. With the bridge shielding them from the view of anyone in the main part of the castle, Keevan pointed upward. Two of his men positioned themselves along the wall and boosted a third man out of the moat. They repeated the action until everyone but Keevan had scrambled out of the moat and lay on their stomachs next to the Tower.

Keevan stepped onto their hands. Dirt crumbled against his fingers when he steadied himself against the bank. The men boosted him upward, and he rolled over the edge onto flat ground.

Frank and Patrick leaned over and yanked the two men up one at a time from the moat.

The five-story Tower speared the sky, blotting out any view of the first evening stars. High on the top floor, Respen was meeting with his Blades. Was Leith Torren already dead? Keevan couldn't feel any urgency for that Blade, but if Torren was dead, then Renna wouldn't be far behind. And Keevan owed Renna for the misery he'd caused her when they were children, and for all the years when she'd unknowingly stayed in Acktar facing the danger meant for him.

Frank slipped past Keevan, pressed against the door to the Tower a moment as if listening, and eased it open.

Keevan followed on his heels, ignoring Patrick's attempt to step in front of him. Inside, two torches burned low in sconces along the wall. Long tables filled the bulk of the room, the benches around them empty.

Frank slunk across the room, sword drawn. At the base of the stairs, he halted and waved Keevan forward. When Keevan reached his side, Frank pointed. "Someone's been here before us."

An eleven-year-old boy, dressed all in black, lay bound and gagged next to the stairs. Rolling over to face them, the boy glared, wiggled, and made a series of muffled yelling noises.

"The rider said the Blade trainee Jamie would try to do what he could to delay Respen." Keevan gripped the hilt of his sword tighter, a chill racing into his fingertips. A boy that young shouldn't look that ready to kill. "Let's keep moving."

He and his men circled the boy and headed up the stairs. Except for the tromp of their boots on stone, the Tower remained silent. Almost dead.

Keevan shivered. Would Respen be at the top? Or was this whole place already abandoned? What if it was a trap and only death waited above?

Still the stairs wound upward into the darkness. Keevan's calves ached with each step. He panted for breath, but he forced himself to keep going.

At this moment, Keevan no longer wanted revenge. He

wasn't even too concerned with justice. He just wanted it over.

On the third floor, he called a halt. It would do them no good to arrive winded to the fight. Respen wouldn't give them time to catch their breath.

Once Keevan could hear his men's breathing over his own, he motioned them for to keep going. He'd dallied long enough. Nearly five years too long.

When they reached the fourth floor, the clash of steel against steel poured down the stairway from the fifth floor.

The fight had started without them.

Keevan broke into a run, taking the stairs two at a time. He hurtled through the open doorway at the top of the stairs and skidded to a halt.

Respen stood against the far wall, knife raised. In front of him, Leith Torren lay bloodied and shaking on the floor, a blond-haired girl bracing herself over his body protecting him from the knife.

Keevan pointed his sword at Respen, knowing that he couldn't get between Renna and the knife in time. If Respen decided to throw it, Keevan's cousin would die. "Drop your knife, Respen Felix. You are under arrest."

Beside Keevan, bows creaked into full draw. Keevan hadn't even realized his men had followed him on his mad dash up the stairs.

Would Respen drop the knife? Perhaps it would be better if he didn't. If he raised it higher and gave Keevan's men a reason to release. It would be a quick and easy end if Respen died right here in the Tower.

Respen's dark eyes lifted to Keevan's. There was something there, like looking into a rattlesnake's eyes the moment before it strikes.

Then Respen's gaze dropped back to Renna. The knife fell from his fingers, striking the floor.

Keevan stared at the knife, lamplight winking along its edges. That's it? He and his men hadn't even had to fight. Could the war have been won in the time it took a knife to fall?

A mass of Blades still struggled against the far wall. Some of them must have joined Torren, but Keevan couldn't tell which ones. He turned to his men. "Tie all the Blades up and lock them in the rooms below."

Soldiers streamed past Keevan, though Brennen and Patrick remained at his side, training bows and arrows at Respen.

Four more men eased past Keevan, ropes in hand, to tie Respen. They circled, making sure they didn't get between Respen and the arrows.

Working his way from the group of Blades, the Blade trainee Jamie Cavendish strode to Keevan and saluted. "Thank you for bringing the army, sir. Those two Blades there, they helped us."

"Understood." Keevan swept his gaze over the two Blades. One was little more than a boy with brown, wavy hair and slim shoulders. He was crying, struggling as Renna knelt beside the body of a Blade. The other Blade Jamie had pointed out stood still as Keevan's soldiers tied his hands. Sweat dampened his curly, blond hair.

There was something about his gaze and his stance. The younger Blade wasn't much of a threat. He was like Jamie, not hardened yet. But Keevan wasn't sure he should trust this older Blade, at least not until he figured out his motives for switching sides at the last minute.

Renna shot to her feet and swept across the room toward him. Blood smeared across her hands and arms, though none of it looked fresh enough to be her own. When she lifted her gaze to his, Keevan caught his breath.

Her eyes, furious and burning as they were now, were Uncle Laurence's eyes.

"Sir, what are you going to do with these two Blades? They fought Respen. They're on the side of the Resistance."

Keevan shook himself. Their first time speaking in nearly six years, and she was asking after those Blades? "They're still Blades. They'll be locked in a cell until a proper inquiry can be held."

It wasn't like they'd joined the Resistance. Keevan couldn't turn them loose without investigating where their true motives and loyalties lay. It wasn't wise.

Renna scowled and shoved a strand of hair out of her face, not even noticing that she'd smeared a streak of blood across her forehead. "Please, at least lock them in a separate cell from the other five Blades. They'll kill Martyn and Ranson if they are locked up together."

"Very well. I'll instruct my men." Keevan gritted his teeth. He should've already thought of that, though he wasn't sure what he was going to do with any of the Blades, on his side or not.

Well, except for the Blade lying on the ground shaking with every breath. Keevan knew what he had to do about him, much as he didn't want to. A promise was a promise.

Renna was still staring at him as if waiting for something. He searched her eyes, but he couldn't see any sort of recognition. Had he really changed so much over the years that Renna would no longer recognize him?

Then again, if Renna hadn't been the only girl in the room, he might not have recognized her either.

"You don't recognize me, do you?" He waited, but after a moment, she shook her head.

What would she think when he told her? He'd tormented her as a child. Maybe it had been childish pranks, but it wouldn't have felt that way to her. She hadn't recoiled when she'd heard the monster rasp to his voice, but would she flinch when she learned he was the cousin who'd been a monster to her?

"I'm your cousin Keevan."

She flinched, and it took all of Keevan's self-control not to wince. Yes, she still remembered. All too well.

The silence tightened, but Keevan didn't dare fill it. Should he apologize for all the things he'd said and done to her years ago? He'd have to someday, but now didn't seem the right time. Not while a war still waged outside this Tower.

She straightened her shoulders as if also deciding there were more important things right now than the past. "I'm glad you're alive. Now, could you spare two of your men? Leith needs to be carried to somewhere I can tend him."

Keevan risked another glance at Torren. Blood pooled on the floor around him, his body so thin his ribs and the sharp points of his elbows jutted against his skin.

Torren's sharp gasps, the blood…it seemed all too familiar from that moonlit night when Keevan had gasped and choked on his own blood, and Torren had fled.

But Torren wasn't that Blade anymore, and Keevan

wasn't that boy. It was time to move on. To give mercy, undeserved as it was.

Because, truthfully, Leith Torren had won the war before Keevan had even stepped a toe in that room.

Keevan waved to Frank and Oran. "Please stay with the lady and aid her as she requires."

Frank nodded. He didn't question why Keevan was placing his own bodyguards in charge of Renna and this wounded Blade, even though Keevan might need men at his side when he tried to end the fighting outside.

But this was the least Keevan could do for Renna to make up for the terror he'd been as a boy.

He'd done all he could for Renna. Now to do his duty for his country. Keevan faced Respen and the four soldiers holding him. "Bring him along. Time to stop this war."

Keevan didn't wait for them to reply. He set out down the stairs he'd sprinted up only minutes ago. Brennen fell into step behind him, but Patrick fell back. When Keevan glanced over his shoulder, Patrick had situated himself behind Respen, his arrow still nocked to the string, though the bow wasn't drawn back. If Respen tried anything, Patrick was ready.

Keevan didn't look back again. He didn't have to. His men were capable enough that they wouldn't let Respen try anything, much less succeed.

When they finally exited the Tower, screaming and shouting and screeching metal cut the air. Were Keevan's soldiers holding their own? If not, Keevan marching out with Respen wouldn't do much good. Respen's army would simply overwhelm Keevan's small group of men and take Respen back, if Patrick didn't put an arrow into him first.

They didn't meet any resistance as they crossed the wooden bridge and entered the passageway connecting Nalgar Castle's two courtyards. To their right, knots of fighting men surged back and forth across the opening into the cobblestone courtyard. In the dark, Keevan couldn't pick out which ones were his men, and which were Respen's.

Instead of trying to push their way into the mob, Keevan led them across the passageway to the narrow, dark stairs leading into the king's chambers. The guards had long since deserted their post to join the fighting.

How many times had Keevan trudged up here as a child, trying to get his father to look up long enough from his paperwork to notice him?

At the top, Keevan took a deep breath and pushed the door open. Much of the room remained as he remembered it. The same burgundy rugs covered the floor with the same dark wainscoting on the walls. The desk had been moved away from the window, though it was the same desk where his father had spent most of his life.

Keevan glanced at the closed door to the bedchamber beyond. Did Respen even sleep in the same bed where he'd murdered Keevan's father? A shudder raced down Keevan's back, and he wasn't sure he wanted to know if Respen was that much of a cold-blooded snake.

His soldiers fanned out. Several of them drifted into the shadows, searching for threats, while others lit the lamps.

"You think you have won." Respen's voice slithered through the darkness behind him.

Keevan turned. Respen stood between two guards, Patrick a few steps behind him. Keevan raised his eyebrows. "Of course. Haven't I?"

A twitch of a smile crossed Respen's face. Keevan gritted his teeth. Respen was captured. His hands bound, an arrow aimed at his back. He shouldn't be smirking.

Respen yanked his arms free of the guards and paced a few steps away, his stride firm, as if he didn't remember the arrow trained on him. "Yes, you have defeated me. You will probably kill me. But how long will you manage to hold on to Acktar? I held it for nearly five years. I doubt you will do any better."

"I'm the Eirdon heir." Keevan fisted his hands at his sides. He shouldn't talk to Respen. He should be above this.

Respen snorted and turned to the window. "You are the scarred son of a pitiful king. Your father was the one who let Acktar fall apart. The people wanted a strong king, and that is what I gave them. But what do they want now? They want revenge, and you will not be able to give it to both sides. This country has only begun to destroy itself, and when it does, you will fall with it."

Was Respen right? Was Keevan's reign already doomed?

He swallowed against the ache in his throat. What if he failed at this too? After all, he had failed at everything else he'd ever done. He'd even failed to die. This time, it wouldn't be one girl who would be hurt. It would be the whole country.

"Keevan?" Brennen nudged his arm.

Keevan shook himself. He couldn't let Respen's words slip into his head. Keevan had four years of practice leading at Eagle Heights. He straightened his back and met Respen's gaze. "That's where you're wrong. The country never wanted strength. They wanted justice. There's a difference."

Pulling his dagger from its sheath, Keevan strode to

Respen, gripped his elbow, and yanked him to the window. Respen didn't resist, even though he stood an inch or two taller than Keevan.

Keevan shoved Respen against the window and pressed the dagger to Respen's throat. Letting go of Respen's arm, he reached past him to unlatch the window and push it open.

The roar of battle pummeled the air. In the faint light coming from the torches spaced along the walls, Keevan could barely make out the tumble of fighting men. "Bring a lamp over here."

Footsteps scuffed behind Keevan, then beams of light burst around him and Respen.

Keevan stared down at the war filling the courtyard below him. Even if his voice hadn't been damaged, he couldn't make a noise loud enough to be heard over that clamor. But now, it would only be pitiful to try.

Something in the movement of the fighting below caught his attention. Did those men have their hands in the air? Parts of the courtyard stilled.

A bugle sounded, and men craned their necks looking for the source. Their faces tipped upward. More of the fighting halted.

Keevan gathered as much breath as he could and put all his strength into a shout. "I am Keevan Eirdon, true prince and heir of Acktar, and I have captured the traitor Respen. All of you who supported Respen, surrender now and you will not be harmed."

Keevan's shout wasn't loud. His voice wasn't strong enough to carry. But, amazingly, the courtyard below him fell into a deep silence, broken only by the ring of swords and knives clattering against the cobblestones as they fell from surrendering hands.

Justice. That was what Keevan had told Respen. The country needed the kind of justice that managed to be both fair and merciful.

As General Stewart had once pointed out, Keevan couldn't execute everyone who'd supported Respen, not without killing half the country. Perhaps it was deserved, but that was where mercy came in.

If Keevan could learn to be merciful to Torren, then surely he could figure out a way to bring the same mercy to the rest of Acktar.

As Keevan swept his gaze over the crowd of faces turned toward him, he didn't see enemies and allies. All he saw were citizens of Acktar. All of them, no matter which side of the war they'd been on, were his people.

He would give them his best. Every part of his heart and soul if he had to.

God willing, it would be enough.

15

Keevan hauled himself to his feet and tottered to the next man in the Great Hall. The wounded men filled the hall, spilling into the cobblestone courtyard. And, like before, Keevan was going to visit each and every one of them.

If only the task didn't seem so endless and Keevan's muscles and eyes weren't so tired.

General Stewart strolled between the rows of men and fell into step with Keevan. "Respen is locked in the North Tower dungeon. Do you want us to imprison Respen's generals and captains there or somewhere else?"

Keevan halted. When his father had been king, the Tower had been the main prison. The North Tower dungeon had only been used for less dangerous criminals. Putting Respen there was bad enough, but putting all his generals and captains in one place where they could possibly plot together...

No, Keevan would rather Respen remain isolated.

"We'll lock them in the Tower. You'll have to search each room to make sure there are no hidden weapons the Blades left behind." Keevan searched the Great Hall until he spotted Renna. "Give me a few minutes first. I'm not sure where Renna left Torren, but we probably should move him before we send men over there."

General Stewart nodded. "Very good, sire."

Keevan picked his way across the room and reached Renna's side as she finished tying off a bandage around a man's abdomen. "Can I speak with you for a moment?"

Renna stood. The rings around her eyes looked nearly as deep as Keevan's.

He lowered his tone, though the wounded men around them were in no shape to eavesdrop. "I plan to use the Tower to imprison Respen's generals and captains, but I believe it would be best if neither my men nor Respen's saw Leith Torren."

Renna scrunched her fingers into the tattered end of her shirt, leaving bloody fingerprints on the fabric. "Leith's resting on a table in the common room. He can be moved, carefully. He has several cracked ribs, and one that's broken all the way. Where would you like to move him to? I probably should go with you. I..."

Her gaze fell to the rows of wounded men still waiting for care. Other healers and volunteers worked among the men, but it wasn't enough. There were too many wounded, and too few healers.

"My men and I can take care of him. We'll move him to a room in the guest apartments."

Renna bit her lip. "Actually, can you move someone else

too? Turns out my sister Brandi joined the army. She's wounded."

Keevan sucked in a breath. He'd failed his cousins yet again. What had Brandi been thinking? Had he really hurt her so badly that she was desperate enough to do this?

This was his fault. So much for being a wise king. He couldn't even be a wise cousin.

"I'll move her too."

"Put them in the same room. It'll be easier for me to care for them." Renna pointed across the Great Hall. "Jamie is sitting next to Brandi."

Keevan spotted Jamie's shaggy brown hair. As he set out across the hall once again, he waved for Patrick and Brennen to join him. They reached his side a few feet away from where Jamie sat next to a still, small form sprawled on the stone floor. A bandage wrapped around the figure's head, and if Renna hadn't told him, Keevan wouldn't have known it was Brandi.

Actually, it looked a lot like the boy message rider from earlier in the evening...the one who'd gone with Jamie...

Keevan folded his arms tightly against his chest. That had been Brandi. No wonder she'd been so insistent that he had to attack tonight.

He couldn't dwell on it. Right now, he had to be a king, and a king didn't have time to grieve or regret too long. Only learn from his mistakes and move on. "Brennen, can you round up some of the men. This boy here," Keevan pointed at Brandi, "needs to be moved to one of the back rooms in the guest wing. Jamie will want to go along. Once you're done, meet me in the Tower."

When Brennen nodded, Keevan headed for the door

leading to the Queen's Court, Patrick at his heels. As he stepped outside, the night drenched him with crisp, fresh air, free of the stench of blood and screams of pain. Far above, a crystalline dome of stars stretched as far and as deep as he could see.

Rounding the corner of the courtyard, Keevan ducked into the passageway and crossed the bridge to the Tower. At the door, he paused. "Stay here. Don't let anyone besides Brennen and his men come in."

Patrick eyed him. "You're going in alone?"

"Frank and Oran should still be in there." Keevan pushed the door open without waiting for Patrick's response.

Oran straightened and saluted as Keevan entered. Frank glanced up, then back down at Torren, who lay on a straw tick on the table behind them.

"Oran, report to the healers in the Great Hall." Keevan approached the table slowly.

Why the urge to have this moment alone? It wasn't like Torren was awake, or Keevan was ready for anything resembling forgiveness yet.

"Frank, can you join Patrick guarding the outside door?" Keevan rested his palms against the table next to Torren. "He can fill you in on what's happening."

Frank crossed his arms. "And leave you alone?"

"I'm safe here."

Yes, safe with the man who'd once sliced Keevan's face and throat. But he was also unconscious and far too hurt to move.

Frank's and Oran's footsteps tromped off and the door shut.

And Keevan was alone with Leith Torren for the first time in nearly five years.

Torren lay on a thin mattress. Bandages covered his torso from below his arms all the way to the waistband of his trousers. Another bandage wrapped around his left thigh, this one soaked with blood. Red welts and gashes peeked over Torren's shoulder. Whiplashes.

Keevan finally understood what the maid Ellenora had seen and meant when she'd faced him only a few weeks ago.

Torren had suffered enough.

Maybe Torren's other victims would want justice done, but Keevan wouldn't ask for anything more.

Torren moaned, and his breathing gasped louder.

Keevan froze. Was Torren waking up? Keevan wasn't sure he was ready to face Torren at this moment.

But Torren's eyes remained pressed closed, tears leaking from the corners.

Keevan let out a long breath. Torren wasn't fully unconscious, but he wasn't going to wake either. He was caught in the between realm of agony, a prison it took hours, sometimes days, to escape, as Keevan remembered too well.

Another moan. Another shuddering breath.

Keevan hung his head, clenching his fingers against the tabletop. If Torren had been any other wounded soldier, Keevan wouldn't hesitate. He would've already offered what little comfort he could.

Why did it have to be Torren?

Sighing, Keevan located a bucket of fresh water left on the table with a tin cup next to it. Dipping the cup in the water, Keevan returned to Torren's side, eased a hand beneath his head, and raised the cup. Keevan dribbled the water into Torren's mouth, waited for him to swallow by reflex, and poured in a few more drops.

Torren's moans and breathing calmed. Keevan set the cup aside and stepped back.

Not a moment too soon. The door swung open, and Frank and Brennen strode in, followed by two more men carrying a stretcher.

Keevan breathed out slowly, strangely thankful he was the only one who would ever remember these last few minutes.

AT THE SOUND OF A RIDER, ADDIE STRUGGLED TO HER FEET. News from the war. Was Keevan alive?

She breathed a prayer, a hand over their unborn child, as the rider slid his horse to a halt in front of the main cabin. He swung down and held out a letter to her. "For you, milady."

Addie heard the footsteps of people gathering around her, but she couldn't look. The papers filled her vision, and her fingers, trembling, were reaching for them even as her heart hammered with the knowledge that the words contained there could build or destroy her life.

She unfolded them. *My dearest Addie...*

Tears pricked her eyes. He was alive.

Firm hands gripped her shoulders. She glanced up at her papa, one of the few men left behind to guard Eagle Heights. "Keevan's alive."

She turned back to Keevan's letter. *I'm alive and unharmed, as are all your brothers, though Samuel was wounded at Walden. We have succeeded in taking Nalgar Castle. By the time you read this, Respen will have been tried and executed.*

Please read the enclosed letter to everyone at Eagle Heights.

Addie switched to the second page and a quick scan told her it was an official announcement. She straightened her shoulders and faced the crowd that had gathered in front of her. No need to call them together. They'd already come, at least those living on the mountaintop. She would have to reread the letter to the villages below later.

With a deep breath, she projected her voice as loudly as she could. "By the good pleasure and grace of God, we have gained the victory."

She had to pause as a cheer rose from the crowd. A release of nearly five years of tension. She couldn't help a smile. Yes, now was the perfect time to cheer.

"We must mourn for those we have lost, but we must also move on to rebuild Acktar. This country has been torn apart by this war. It would be easy to hang on to the bitterness and hatred that war has caused. But we must let go of our hatred and forgive. It is the only way we can reconcile one half of this nation with the other. Healing will take time, but I believe it is possible."

Addie let Keevan's words soak into her. Forgiveness. Healing. That's what Keevan had needed, and it was now what this country needed.

And he couldn't do it alone. He needed her.

Addie's grip tightened on the papers in her hand. She had to be at Keevan's side right now. For the past two years, she hadn't been quite sure what it meant to be his princess and future queen. The titles hadn't held much weight at Eagle Heights.

But Keevan was about to become king. And he needed her at his side. It was something they should do together.

"Papa." Addie turned. "Can you saddle a horse for me? I'm going to join Keevan."

"Addie." Papa stared, his big hands loose at his sides. "It's too far. And you don't even know the way."

"He can take me." Addie pointed at the rider. She turned to Mama, who threaded her arm through Papa's. "The baby won't be born for another month and a half yet. Tell him, Mama. I'll be fine. We'll take it slow, as slow as I need to. But I have to go to Nalgar Castle. Keevan can't do this alone."

Mama studied her, then patted Papa's arm. "We'll all go."

Over Mama's shoulder, Addie's sister-in-law Suzanne gripped her three-year-old and one-year-old sons tighter, her chin raising slightly. Penelope planted her hands on her hips while Juliana stepped closer.

Addie smiled. Yes, they would all go. And they would all stand with Keevan.

KEEVAN SAT BEHIND THE DESK IN THE KING'S CHAMBERS. THE same desk where his father used to sit. The same one where Respen had sat only a week before.

The patch of sky visible through the window remained black with nighttime clouds. The lone candle shone an orange glow across the papers scattered on the desk.

Only one signed and sealed paper lay off to the side. The order for Respen's execution, to be carried out in the morning. That had been the easy piece of paperwork.

Keevan fingered the corner of the sheet of paper in front

of him. *I, Keevan Eirdon, rightful and recognized heir of the throne of Acktar, hereby pardon the man Leith Torren, former Blade under the traitor Respen Felix, for all the crimes committed under said traitor's commands...*

He'd been trying for the past hour, but he couldn't bring himself to sign and seal it. Once he did that, it would be official.

Was this the right thing to do? Keevan would deny justice to Torren's victims.

When Shadrach had defended Torren, he'd only had to do it in front of Keevan. If Keevan signed this pardon, he would have to defend Torren against the whole country. No, more than that, Keevan would have to balance his throne and future on the sword's edge for Torren.

Would Torren be worth it?

Shadrach believed he was. As did Lord Alistair.

If Keevan signed and sealed that pardon, he would have to believe it too.

His gaze landed on the other stack of papers. Letters to the families of every man killed fighting for Keevan. They had given their all for him, and a personal letter was the least he could do.

Even if writing the words *To the family of Ian McCrae* to the family of a dead fourteen-year-old boy, hurt as much as cutting open his own heart and bleeding onto the page.

If Torren hadn't turned himself in, if he and the Blades who'd joined him hadn't managed to subdue Respen and the Blades so that Keevan could end the battle that much quicker, how many more fourteen-year-old boys would've died? How many more letters would Keevan have had to write then?

To be honest, and Keevan really didn't want to be honest about this, Leith Torren had saved Acktar.

And for that, what else could Keevan do?

He pushed to his feet, unable to sit still any longer. But pacing back and forth by the window didn't help. This was about more than just Torren. It was about Keevan's reign. What kind of king would he be? How would he balance justice and mercy?

Slumping back in his chair, Keevan reached for his Bible next to the candle. The book already lay open, revealing tattered pages and a verse heavily underlined in ink. *The king's heart is in the hand of the Lord.*

Keevan had read this part of the Bible so many times, he had all the stories memorized. David, a man after God's own heart, but also a man who'd fallen much as Keevan had. Solomon, so wise, yet so foolish in wandering away from God near the end of his life. All the kings of those Bible stories who had known the truth but only a handful truly believed and walked in it.

If those kings had struggled to both follow God and be good kings, then how much hope did Keevan have? Was it even possible to be both a good Christian and a good king, especially a king over a country where half the people didn't have the same beliefs he did? Keevan had to be both just and merciful to all of them, regardless of belief. No, more than that, Keevan was determined to be just and merciful because of his own beliefs.

Keevan read the verse again. He had to commit his heart, life, and reign to God's hands, not his own.

Folding his hands, Keevan leaned his head on his fingers.

Heavenly Father, grant me the wisdom to rule this country. But more than wisdom, keep my heart humble.

Opening his eyes, Keevan pulled the pardon toward him, picked up his pen, and scrawled his signature at the bottom of the page.

16

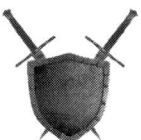

Traveling for more than two weeks in the saddle while nearly eight months pregnant was about the worst thing Addie had ever experienced, except for the night she'd pressed her fingers to the gaping wound in Keevan's neck.

But the moment Nalgar Castle peeked over the horizon, it was all worth it.

If Addie had been a little less pregnant, she would've kicked the horse into a gallop down the hill to the gate. Instead, she focused on keeping the horse to a walk.

Last time she'd seen Nalgar, she'd ridden away in the middle of the night, a bleeding Prince Keevan held on the saddle in front of her.

Now it was midday, a washed-out summer sun bulging in the sky. The Eirdon banner, a silver cross against a light green background, flapped over each tower. And somewhere in that castle, Addie's husband was waiting to become king.

At the gate, they reined in their horses. Papa turned to Addie. "It's your castle."

Addie stared upward at the soldiers leaning over the battlements. She cupped her hands over her mouth. "Open up for Princess Adelaide Eirdon."

The soldiers above straightened so fast one of them nearly tripped. The gates swung open, and Addie urged her horse forward into the tunnel through the wall.

As she broke into the sunshine on the other side, squinting, a figure burst from the passageway. Addie barely had time to blink before Keevan was at her horse's side, gaping up at her. "Addie! What are you...how..."

"I had to come." Addie forced herself to grin. "Now get me off this horse."

Addie ran her fingers over the tabletop, its surface extended as far as possible, with extra chairs crowded around it. Another two end tables had been added to either side. Still, it would be crowded once her whole family got here.

Her gaze snagged on the door across the way, the one leading to the bedchamber. That's where Respen had slept. She shivered. Would she and Keevan now share that room? It didn't seem right to sleep in the same place where that... that monster had also slept.

"What do you think?" Keevan rested his hands on her shoulders, leaning over to place a kiss on her hair.

"It's...different than our cabin." Addie couldn't face Keevan. She didn't want to disappoint him.

"But this place reeks of Respen. Even after he's been dead and buried for weeks." Keevan rubbed her shoulders. "I've been staying in my old room. I'm thinking about turning these rooms into offices for the king's clerks."

"And the clerks' offices in the north wall?" Addie tipped her head back to look at him. The afternoon sun shone along the length of his scar.

Keevan grinned. "Room for a library. Maybe a few other things. I'm sure we'll think of something. Do you think Papa would like to be in charge of all that? Chief Carpenter, or whatever title I come up with."

"He'd love it. You know Papa. He would never stay idle when there's work to be done. He and Mama both." Addie leaned her head against the back of her chair.

"I know. I thought about giving your parents land and a title. They are the in-laws of the king, after all." Keevan folded his arms on the back of Addie's chair, his face tipped down so only a few inches separated them.

Addie meant to laugh, but it came out a snort. "They would've hated that."

Keevan straightened and swiped at his face, as if Addie had spewed spit when she'd laughed. She didn't apologize, and he didn't mention it. He returned to his place leaning against the back of her chair. "Do you think Mama would like to be the housekeeper here at Nalgar?"

Addie nearly snorted in Keevan's face again. "All those maids and cooks to boss around? She'd love it. Any plans for the rest of my family? I know Penelope has her sights set on something a little higher than a scullery maid."

"Not sure about Samuel and Juliana. Brennen, I think, would do well as the head stablehand. Penelope...I'm not sure. Think she'd like to be a clerk? I'm sure there'll be a few openings once I go through the administrative staff. Most of them used to work for my father. They did their job, and Respen kept them on." Keevan shrugged. "I'm not sure how many of them I trust."

"Penelope would like that." Addie sighed and shifted her head to more comfortably rest against Keevan's arms.

"She'll probably have every unattached nobleman in Acktar after her, wanting to be brother-in-law to the king. Your papa and brothers are going to have their hands full."

Addie closed her eyes. After the long ride, she might just fall asleep in this chair before her family ever gathered for supper. "I don't think we have to worry too much about her. She's too smart to settle for the first nobleman that comes around with fancy words. Papa and Mama raised us better than that."

"I'm thankful they did."

Keevan's voice rasped near Addie's ear, but she didn't open her eyes. "So that leaves Frank and Patrick. What about them?"

She sensed Keevan straighten. "The army has always handled security at Nalgar, and the duty fell to whatever ranking captain happened to be stationed here. It was a bit haphazard at best. I'd like to make a more permanent security detail whose sole purpose is to guard Nalgar Castle, and specifically the royal family. I'm planning to ask Frank to lead it, and Patrick to back him up. If Frank doesn't want to return to his position as your father's apprentice, of course."

"Frank's seen too much now, and he's always been protective. Taking care of the security for the whole castle sounds like just the job for him. He'd probably do it anyway." Addie peeled her eyes open.

This was Keevan's greatest fear, even more than losing his voice permanently. That someday what had happened to his parents and his brothers could happen to them. Keevan would do his utmost to prevent it.

Keevan's hands rested on Addie's shoulders, his thumbs rubbing at the back of her neck. "Would you rather get some sleep? Your family would understand."

It was tempting. The next few days would be filled with meeting his cousin Renna and the coronation and settling into a new home at Nalgar.

"I'll manage to stay awake." Addie forced herself to sit up a bit straighter. "Besides, I'm not sure I'm ready to be in that room alone yet. You nearly died there. Surely it bothers you too, with that Blade Leith Torren in a room just across the courtyard."

She shivered. She could still feel Keevan's blood pumping through her fingers, hot and sticky, while he choked for each breath.

"All of these rooms have memories. My brothers died in the rooms next to mine. My parents died in that room over there." Keevan tilted his head toward the door. "We can't leave every room in this castle empty. We'll have to fill them with so much happiness the past won't matter. Besides, I might've nearly died in that room, but it's also where I met you."

Keevan's grin had her grinning back. How many times had she seen him relaxed and smiling like this?

Not nearly enough.

"You're rather happy today." Addie reached up and tugged on his arm.

"You're here. We're safe." Keevan wrapped his arms around her, leaning his chin on her head. "Of course I'm happy."

The door rattled, and a whole herd of feet pounded inside. Keevan's sigh whispered through her hair before he straightened.

Yes, they would fill Nalgar with happiness. So much happiness the shadows and ghosts wouldn't stand a chance and the stones of this castle would nearly burst trying to contain it.

K‍EEVAN KEPT HIS PACE MEASURED AS HE STRODE DOWN THE long aisle in the Great Hall, benches on either side filled with soldiers and nobles. All of the attendees were standing, bowing and curtsying as Keevan and Addie passed.

At the far end of the Hall, an organist pounded away at a swelling melody while someone, probably her young son or daughter, pumped the bellows in the back room. A few yards in front of the organ, Lord Conree of Surgis and Lord Segon of Uster, voted by the Gathering of Nobles to be their representatives for the occasion, stood between two small tables.

One table, draped in green silk, held Acktar's crown, a gold band etched with scenes of Acktar's history and emblazoned with a cross at the center of the forehead. A simpler crown sat next to it for Addie. On the other table, a Bible rested on silver silk.

Addie squeezed his arm tighter. He patted her fingers. They could do this. Together.

They halted at the front of the Great Hall, and the music rose into a crescendo. When it ceased, Keevan's ears still rang and ached all the way down into his jaw.

This was the moment they were supposed to kneel. Keevan turned to Addie and helped her ease onto the floor. Her mouth twitched with a grimace, then a smile, and he had to fight his own smile remembering Addie's grumbling during their rehearsal the day before. This ceremony, not to mention the billows of Addie's skirt and the trailing robe, were not designed with eight-month pregnant women in mind.

But as much as she'd grumbled, she was still here. She'd endured two weeks of hard travel to kneel at his side now. Perhaps no one would ever appreciate the kind of queen they had, but he would.

After Keevan knelt next to Addie, Lord Conree picked up the Bible, opened it to the passage Keevan had marked beforehand, and held it out. Pressing his right palm to his chest, Keevan rested his left hand on the Bible.

Lord Conree's tenor rose above the hushed crowd. "Do you, Prince Keevan Eirdon, solemnly swear to perform faithfully your duties as King of Acktar, to defend her borders, provide justice to her citizens, and uphold her laws and regulations to the utmost of your ability, so help you God?"

Keevan swallowed. God had spared him for this moment, but would Keevan be enough? Or would he fail like his father had?

His gaze landed on the verse he'd underlined so many

years ago, now barely visible beneath his fingers. *By me kings reign, and princes decree justice.*

Keevan wasn't enough. Kings that thought they were enough all by themselves fell into pride and tyranny, like Respen.

But Keevan's heart was in the hand of his God. And God was enough.

"I do." He prayed a silent prayer of thanks when his voice remained steady, despite the rasp.

Lord Conree turned to Addie, and she put her left hand on the Bible and her right on her heart like Keevan had.

"Do you, Princess Adelaide Eirdon, solemnly swear to perform faithfully your duties as Queen of Acktar, to stand by her king, provide justice to her citizens, and uphold her laws and regulations to the utmost of your ability, so help you God?"

Addie's fingers quivered on the Bible. "I do."

As Lord Conree stepped back and returned the Bible to its table, Lord Segon picked up the large gold crown and raised it above Keevan's head. "With the power vested in me as the representative of the Gathering of Nobles, I crown you, King Keevan Eirdon of Acktar. May your reign be long, your justice compassionate, and your mercy fair."

Keevan closed his eyes as the cool metal slid over his head and came to rest against his forehead. The muscles at the back of his neck cramped with its weight.

After nearly five years of exile, he was king of Acktar.

Keevan could never forget what that meant. The blood that had been shed and the lives paid to purchase this crown.

He opened his eyes in time to see Lord Segon repeat his

proclamation and slide the second crown onto Addie's head. Her brown curls puffed and frizzed outward from its confines.

When both Lord Segon and Lord Conree bowed, Keevan clambered to his feet, nearly stumbled on his long, light green robe streaming out behind him, and turned to Addie. Gripping her hands, he hauled her to her feet. Together, they faced the crowd.

To one side, a clerk unrolled a piece of paper. "Lord Segon of Uster."

Lord Segon knelt in front of Keevan. "On behalf of the town of Uster, I pledge to you my loyalty and service, my king."

Keevan touched Lord Segon's shoulder in acknowledgement. When Lord Segon rose, Lord Conree took his place, and they repeated the process.

Two towns done. Almost forty to go.

Keevan tried to pay attention as each lord or lady pledged their loyalty. Lord Philip Creston of Arroway, Lord Doughtry of Calloday, Lady Emilin of Dently...on and on.

Lord Norton of Kilm knelt in front of Keevan and gave his pledge of loyalty without hesitation. Though, there was a gleam to his eyes, a twist to his mouth, that sent a chill into Keevan's toes. Lord Norton might pledge his loyalty to Keevan, but he'd once pledged loyalty to Keevan's father, only to join with Respen a few years later.

Lord Alistair's name was called. He stood and strode down the center aisle, his gait still shaky and his left arm limp in its sling. When he bowed and gave his pledge, Keevan touched his shoulder and whispered, "thank you."

After everything Lord Alistair had sacrificed and done to win Keevan this crown, those two words were little thanks.

Lord Alistair straightened and gave Keevan one, small nod, as if they were all the thanks Lord Alistair needed.

Lord Beregern of Mountainwood, a gray-haired man about Lord Alistair's age, knelt and gave his pledge. Another one of Respen's supporters.

Keevan couldn't hold that against them. Not when half the nobles pledging their loyalty to him had once betrayed his father to side with Respen. But Keevan would be cautious. Trust would be hard to regain.

"Lady Rennelda Faythe of Stetterly."

Renna slid to her feet and swept down the aisle, her long blond hair gleaming with the sunshine streaming through the tall, upper windows. When she knelt, her voice remained stronger than Keevan would've expected, and, for a moment, he could see some of Uncle Laurence's steel in her. "On behalf of the town of Stetterly, I pledge to you my loyalty and service, my king."

Keevan touched her shoulder, and as she turned to go, Keevan found himself reaching out and gripping her shoulders, hearing again Uncle Laurence's request to send her to safety, Lord Alistair's pleas for the same.

Yet, Renna had been forced to stay and take the dangers meant for him.

He pitched his rasp low so only she could hear. "Thank you for keeping Acktar's hope alive for so long."

She smiled and patted his hand. "No, thank you for being alive. There was a time I feared I'd end up with the crown."

Keevan released Renna, watching as she returned to her

seat. He still didn't know how he was going to deal with having Renna fall in love with Leith Torren. If they got married, Keevan's almost-killer would become his cousin.

At least Stetterly was a six-day ride away from Nalgar Castle. Family gatherings wouldn't happen too often.

Addie squeezed his hand, and Keevan tilted his head enough to share a look and a smile.

The herald cleared his throat and bellowed in a voice now scratchy from all the shouting he'd done, "General Uriah Stewart, please step forward."

Keevan shook himself and smiled as General Stewart stood and strode down the length of the Great Hall. The years had turned General Stewart's hair gray and lined his face, but he was still the captain that had stood by Keevan during the worst moment of his life.

Many deserved recognition for their actions in the days following Respen's attack. But Keevan couldn't think of anyone he'd rather reward than General Stewart.

General Stewart knelt, a wrinkle forming between his eyes.

Keevan rested a hand on his shoulder. "Nearly five years ago, you saved my life and, having done that, you willingly went into exile with me. You stayed by my side, gave me victory, and returned my country to me. For your loyalty and dedication, I name you the lord of Blathe. May you and your descendants rule that town well."

The reward carried as much of a burden as a gift. Blathe was a rough town, ruled by Respen Felix before being essentially leaderless and abandoned when Respen moved to Nalgar.

But if General Stewart—no, Lord Stewart—could

counsel and prod and nudge a reluctant prince into a king, he could handle Blathe.

"Thank you, Your Majesty." Lord Stewart's bow lowered further. "On behalf of the town of Blathe, I pledge to you my loyalty and service."

And, of all the pledges Keevan had heard that day, this one was the most sincere.

One year. That's how long Respen had predicted it would take for Keevan to fail and the nation to split in two once again.

That year started now.

EPILOGUE

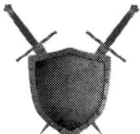

THREE WEEKS LATER...

Keevan rocked his newborn son Duncan in his cradle with a toe and glanced over at Addie. He had to shout to be heard over their son's wails. "He doesn't seem to like it."

"So far, he hasn't liked anything." Addie wrinkled her nose and pushed herself onto her elbows to see. "Hand him back to me. See if that helps."

Keevan eased both hands around Duncan's small body. So small and delicate. And with such healthy, well-functioning lungs. "Do you think we should fetch the midwife again?"

Addie took Duncan from Keevan and cradled him against her. "She said that as far as she could tell, Duncan was simply angry. Hopefully." Addie's forehead puckered as she stroked Duncan's nearly bald head, the baby's face red with all his crying.

Keevan didn't know much about babies, but did they always scream at the top of their lungs for the first hour after they were born? No one, not Addie or Mama or any of Addie's siblings, had been able to get the newborn Prince Duncan to stop crying.

After a few minutes of talking and soothing, Duncan still hadn't stopped. Keevan reached for Duncan again. "Here. Let me take him. I know you need to rest."

Addie passed the baby back to him, and Keevan eased to his feet. If he paced the hallway, maybe Addie could at least get some sleep.

Tucking Duncan against his chest, Keevan strode out the door into the hallway. Moonlight streamed through the windows at the far end and puddled on the floor.

He was halfway down the hall when Duncan finally gave a shudder and lapsed into hiccupping breaths. By the time Keevan reached his door, Duncan's steady, sleepy breathing wafted against his neck. But as soon as he halted, Duncan stirred.

Looked like pacing was the answer. Keevan strolled down the length of the corridor once again, his son a warm, tiny bundle against his chest and neck.

His son. With tiny little fingers and toes and squinched up eyes and such vulnerability that Keevan's heart was destroyed and remade and destroyed again every time he looked at him.

Failing the country would be bad enough, but failing his son? Keevan couldn't let himself think it.

Instead, he cradled his son and paced the corridor long into the night.

Addie was alive. Duncan was healthy. Keevan had a family.

And it was all more than enough.

FREE STORY!

Deal
A Blades of Acktar Short Story

Once there was a nine-year-old boy Leith Torren who only wanted to bring food home to his mother...and was noticed by Lord Respen Felix of Blathe.

Free for newsletter subscribers. Sign up at https://triciamingerink.com/my-newsletter/

ALSO BY TRICIA MINGERINK

DAGGER'S SLEEP

A prince cursed to sleep.
A princess destined to wake him.
A kingdom determined to stop them.

High Prince Alexander has been cursed to a sleep like unto death, a curse that will end the line of the high kings and send the Seven Kingdoms of Tallahatchia into chaos. With his manservant to carry his luggage and his own superior intelligence to aid him, Alex sets off to find one of the Fae and end his curse one way or another.

A hundred years later, Princess Rosanna learns she is the princess destined by the Highest King to wake the legendary sleeping prince. With the help of the mysterious Daemyn Rand, can she find the courage to finish the quest as Tallahatchia wavers on the edge of war?

One curse connects them. A hundred years separate them. From the rushing rivers of Tallahatchia's mountains to the hall of the Highest King himself, their quests will demand greater sacrifice than either of them could imagine.

For readers of adventure, fairy tales, and stirring allegories comes this fresh imagining of the classic Sleeping Beauty tale, the first book in a new YA fantasy series from Tricia Mingerink

Buy Now!

BOOKS BY TRICIA MINGERINK

The Blades of Acktar

Dare

Deny

Defy

Destroy: A novella

Deliver

Decree

Beyond the Tales

Dagger's Sleep

Midnight's Curse

Poison's Dance

Goose Princess

ACKNOWLEDGMENTS

Thank you for taking the time to read this novella. Even if it isn't about Leith and Renna, I hope you still loved the characters and connected with their struggles.

Thank you especially to those who submitted names for *Defy*. I didn't use your names then, but I kept them and used them for this book instead. Thank you to Kim Moss for the name Arlo, Paul Ophoff for Brennan, which I changed to Brennen. Molly M. for the name Conree, Gabriela Paige for Kester and Oran, and Mandy Steinberger for Theodor and Thadius.

A special thank you to my brother Andy for the names Frank and Patrick.

Thanks to my family and friends for understanding when I disappeared during the month of November to finish this novella.

A big hug for all my author friends, especially Jaye who helped encourage me when I ran stuck on how to present the themes in this book, Nadine for asking for this novella during her edit of *Defy*, and Katie and Ashley for word wars early in NaNo when I wrote most of the ending of this novella. All of you guys are the absolute best!

To Sierra, for your last minute critique of *Destroy* that helped give it that final polish!

Thank you also to a few of my early readers who found a few missing words and typos.

But most of all, thanks to my Heavenly Father who always is and shall be enough.

Printed in Great Britain
by Amazon

25c44341-2361-480a-84a8-cc11983ae495R01